EVERLASTING CIRCLE

THE EVERLAST SERIES BOOK 4

JULIANA HAYGERT

COPYRIGHT

This book is a work of fiction. Names, characters, places, and incidents either are products of the author's imagination or are used fictitiously. Any resemblance to actual persons, living or dead, events, or locales is entirely coincidental.

Manufactured in the United States of America.

First Edition June 2016

Second Edition January 2018

www.JulianaHaygert.com

Edited by H. Danielle Crabtree

Proofreading by Running Ink Edits

Cover design by Moonchildljilja at <u>Fantasy Book Design</u>

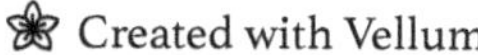 Created with Vellum

LIST OF DEITIES

Mani – Fate (past)
Nay – Fate (present)
Lavni – Fate (future)

Levi – God of balance, life, and spirit
Ceris – Goddess of love, family, home, and beauty
Mitrus – God of death, dead, and underworld
Omi – God of war
Imha – Goddess of chaos
Sol – God of sun and day
Lua – Goddess of moon and night
Izaera – Goddess of nature and seasons
Ronen – Goddess of entertainment
Maho – God of magic

Keisha – hero
Alice – hero
Zelen – a forest protector

Akuma – giant bat-like demons
Ornek – wingless demons
Arak – wingless demons

Amiel, Jed, Dane, Riel, Deven, Keon, Eklan, and Chael – Death Lords

Rihan, Tuzin, Nyria, and Letos – scouts
Corinia – lesser goddess under Maho
Aruhi – lesser god under Ceris
Edan and Nuri – lesser god and goddess under Sol

1

NADINE

THREE WEEKS, TWO DAYS, EIGHT HOURS, AND FORTY-SEVEN minutes.

That was how long Micah had been gone. But who was counting? Not me. Because I didn't care. Not anymore.

Or so I told myself.

Instead of obsessing about why he left with no explanation, I immersed myself in training with Keisha, planning with Ceris, and learning more about the creed with Victor—though he warned me that not even he remembered all the stories and legends. Meanwhile, Ceris had found four deities to work as scouts—Rihan, Tuzin, Nyria, and Letos, who would spy on Imha's and Omi's activities. Izaera and Zelen spent several days at a time away looking for more forest protectors, nymphs, or any kind of nature-related deities to join our group. Ceris called it an army, but we were only seven so far. Seven wasn't an army.

I tried to focus on each step I took, but it never worked. Instead, my mind always got away from me when I was running. It was hard to believe all that had happened in the last six months. I had found Victor, the guy I had been having visions of for ten months, and Micah, a guy I didn't see coming but who rocked my world. Then, I found out they were actually gods—Micah was Mitrus, the god of death and the dead and the underworld, and Victor was Levi, the god of balance, life, and spirit. Even worse was to find out a good friend of mine, Cheryl, was actually a goddess in disguise and had manipulated my life for almost a year. She had even manipulated my feelings for Victor, making me crazy about him, just to snatch him from me in the end. And there was so much more ... we found Morgan, a high priest, and Keisha, a freaking hero. We encountered Imha and Omi more times than I dared to admit, and they even captured and tortured me ... and killed my family. We had been betrayed and hurt and broken apart one too many times. But we were still here, fighting against the darkness Imha and Omi had unleashed upon our world.

I had been running on the treadmill for seventy-three minutes when an idea popped in my head. Why hadn't I thought of it before? Ceris wanted an army? Maybe I could give her one.

I stopped the treadmill and jumped off it.

"What is it?" Keisha asked, mildly out of breath from running on the treadmill beside mine. Her dark skin glistened with sweat, and her long black ponytail bounced side to side.

"Just ... need to see something." I grabbed the towel from the treadmill and dabbed my damp face.

I walked into the living room, still finding it odd not seeing Zelen seated on the floor, praying. The air here smelled faintly of lavender. Ceris had made it her mission to prevent the foul air outside from entering the apartment, so she kept scented candles lit all the time in all the rooms.

After I quickly washed my hands and face in the half-bath adjacent to the apartment's foyer, I went back to the living room. Where would Ceris have put it? I searched the TV stand, the shelves, under the coffee table. I moved on to the dining room, our usual meeting room, and searched the buffet cabinet and inside the many books Ceris had brought from all over the world that were crowding the dining room. The walls were lined with books—sans-shelves—sorted in piles as high as my chest. Nothing in here either.

I considered the kitchen, but Ceris wouldn't have hidden it in the kitchen. Where else then? I wouldn't search her bedroom.

"What are you looking for?" Ceris asked from behind me.

I turned to her. As usual, her sight made me self-conscious. She was a goddess—the goddess of love, family, home, and beauty—and she was stunning. Her long white hair fell down her back like a cascade of silver, her clear blue eyes shone with power, her skin was smooth, unblemished, and her figure ... well, she was a goddess.

"The map," I answered.

She extended her hand between us and the rolled map appeared in her outstretched palm. "Here." I took it from her, sat on the couch, and unrolled the yellowed map with torn edges on the coffee table. Ceris sat beside me. "What are you looking for?"

The bright symbols came to life on the paper, sprouting all around the map. They didn't rush around like the first time I had seen them. This time most of them were still in their places, some shining brighter than the others.

"What are the other gods' symbols?" I asked.

"You're going to try to find them?" Victor asked, entering the living room.

I looked up and nodded. His beauty didn't have the same effect on me as it had when we first met, but I couldn't deny he was handsome. Gorgeous even. With honey-colored hair, sea-green eyes, fair skin, a chiseled face, and a tall, strong figure, who wouldn't think he was gorgeous? Moreover, he was a god. His power was as tangible and suffocating as Ceris's.

"That's a good idea," Ceris said.

She produced a book with a worn leather cover out of thin air. *The Gods and Goddess of the Everlasting Circle*. Ugh, I knew this book. I had skimmed through it less than two months ago. It belonged to Morgan, a high priest. He was now in the underworld, and I had put him there.

The hurt snaked its way into my chest. It hit fast and hard, and it became difficult to breathe. Just like every night when I woke up from the same nightmare.

"Nadine?" Victor asked. He sat on the arm of the sofa beside Ceris.

I shook that feeling aside—just aside, because it never left me—took the book from Ceris and opened to the chapters about the other gods and goddesses—Sol, god of the sun and day; Lua, goddess of the moon and night; Ronen, goddess of entertainment and arts; and Maho, god of magic—and tried to memorize their symbols. All of the major gods and goddess symbols were encased in a circle, so it was easy to distinguish from the rest. I couldn't find Sol's symbol, Lua's and Ronen's kept flashing all over the map, but Maho's was strong and on a little island in Thailand.

I pressed the tip of my index finger on the map. "This is Maho. He must be there."

"The Phi Phi Islands, of course," Victor said, leaning over the map. "We should go there."

"Now?" Ceris asked. "But Izaera and Zelen aren't here. It would be only the four of us, and …" She paused, looking at me.

"And I count for almost nothing?" I replied, being careful not to show how much her comments hurt sometimes. "I know, but that's what you got."

"We can go scout the place," Victor said, trying to appease Ceris. "If we see it's clear, we proceed. If there are demons or trouble, we fall back and summon Izaera and Zelen."

I sighed. If Micah were here, we would have three full gods instead of two. But he wasn't, and I had to accept that. Why was it so hard, damn it?

Ceris sighed. "All right. Let's go."

I stood and inhaled deeply. One more step toward the end.

The end. Soon it would be the end of the war. We would win—I had to believe that—and end thirty years of darkness, or we would lose, leaving Imha and Omi to reign over the world, spreading chaos and terror.

Regardless of the outcome, my end would come. That was, of course, if Micah returned to finish our deal.

2

MICAH

"More, my lord?" the red-haired girl asked. She knelt on the edge of my black chaise lounge and ran a finger over my bare chest.

"Yes," I said, my voice low.

Wearing a seductive smile, she stepped away from the chaise lounge and strolled to the bar on my right. She poured me another double shot of whiskey, while the other girls—a blonde, a brunette, a black, and an Asian one—danced three feet from me. Danced was a nice way to put it. Dressed in nothing more than scant tops covering only their nipples and long, flowy skirts with several slits from top to bottom, they kissed and touched each other, moving their hips as if they couldn't wait to get some.

For a few seconds, I became aroused and considered joining them.

But only for a few seconds.

Then the memories came crashing over me, and I sat there, staring at the crystal chandelier on the ceiling, not acknowledging the dancers.

The memories …

The Soul Oath, the Cup of Life, my Dark Lords' betrayal … my helplessness.

I looked down at the black web on my left chest where the Black Thorn had broken my skin and spread its poison. I had lived, but I didn't know for how much longer. In the past three weeks, the tendrils had grown an inch or so.

Would it keep spreading? If they did, what would happen when they covered every inch of my skin? Would the poison finally kill me? What if my soul didn't find a host this time? And what if it did? Would I grow up with another family in this dark world? By then, Imha and Omi would have destroyed everything. There would be no hosts to take me.

I picked up a shirt from the hardwood floor and was about to pull it over my head to hide the black web when the red-haired girl came back with my drink.

She bowed. "Is there anything else I can do for you, my lord?" I took my drink and shook my head. "Are you sure?" she asked, gesturing to the other girls.

They stopped dancing and stepped aside, revealing a new girl in their midst. A girl who haunted my dreams and nightmares. A girl who didn't leave my mind even during the waking hours. A girl who was too much for me, and yet, I couldn't stop desiring her.

Nadine.

She stared at me with her big green eyes, her red lips pulling into a naughty smirk. Her long brown hair fell into waves down her back, her flawless skin shone, and her body … my gods, her lean body looked fantastic in the scant top and flowy skirt.

My heart stuttered, and I sat up.

She strolled to me, her hips swishing, her smile widening. By the gods, she was so beautiful it hurt.

Without a word, she knelt on the chaise and crawled over me. I lay back down as she straddled me, placing her hips right above mine and resting her hands on my chest.

I sucked in a sharp breath.

This woman would be the death of me.

"Kiss me," she whispered, leaning into me.

Hell, yeah.

I ran my hands over the smooth skin of her waist, up her back, until I was cupping her neck and pulling her down to me.

Something squeaked to my right.

I snapped my head to the side and saw Rok catching a rat in the corner of the room.

The illusion broke, and I looked around at the shitty motel room. There weren't any hardwood floors, or velvet chaises, or crystals chandeliers, or bars filled with drinks, or sexy dancers.

Or Nadine.

It had been a hallucination. The fourth one this week.

I stared at the half-empty bottle of whiskey in my hand. I didn't know if the constant booze was responsible for the hallucinations, or if it was my tricky mind, my desire, or my powers. I didn't care either.

As much as I loved daydreaming about Nadine, it wasn't helping.

I shot up from the moldy mattress on the ratty twin bed and threw the bottle at the wall. The glass shards and the rest of the liquid splashed everywhere. A large piece fell next to my bare feet.

I crouched down and closed my hand around it,

squeezing as hard as I could. Blood seeped from my fist and pain spread through my body. I gritted my teeth and welcomed it. The pain would wake me up and keep me on my toes.

The pain would knock some sense into me.

I let out a long breath.

It was time to stop running—or stop looking for the Death Lords. I didn't think I had the courage to face Nadine yet, but I couldn't sit here and wait for the Cup of Life to appear in front of me. I had to do something.

I picked up my shirt from the chaise and pulled it over my head. Then I put on my boots and leather jacket. I probably looked like shit but didn't really care. The one person who might make me want to look presentable wouldn't see me anytime soon.

"You know what to do," I said to Rok. He let out a short squawk and went back to his rat.

I left a few bills on the bed to pay for the room, and then teleported out of there.

The world spun around me before settling in the luscious room of my illusions. Only this one wasn't an illusion. This was one of the rooms in my corner of the underworld—my own little palace—the only place where no one else could find me unless I wanted them too.

I should have come here weeks ago, right after I left Nasya's island. I hadn't though. I hadn't because here I was the almighty god of death and the dead. Here, I was the leader. And nothing reminded me more that I had failed than being in a position of leadership.

I dropped on the chaise lounge, a real one, and exhaled.

I was tired. Tired of being tough, tired of running, tired of pretending.

Feeling all crappy and emotional, a sudden wish to talk to someone hit me strong and hard. But who could I talk to? Levi was the first one that came to mind. He had always been my brother and best friend, even when we didn't always see eye to eye. But that meant returning to NYC, and I wasn't ready. Not yet.

Then I remembered someone who was here in the underworld, and I could easily summon him with a snap of my fingers. Which was exactly what I did.

Morgan appeared in front me. He looked around, his eyes wide. "What ...? Where ...?" Then he saw me, and his eyes widened more. "My lord." He knelt in front of me, his head low. "My lord, forgive me. By the Everlast, my lord, I had no idea what I was doing. I didn't think the dagger would influence me, and I still can't believe my will was so weak. Please, forgive me, my lord. I beg you, I—"

"Shut up, Morgan," I snapped. He closed his mouth and kept his head low. "I know all that. I know you would never willingly betray us."

He peeked at me from behind his hair. "You do?"

I nodded. "Don't worry. I didn't summon you to judge you."

"Then why did you summon me, my lord?"

"Because ..." I poured whiskey into two glasses, gritting my teeth. I couldn't believe I would say it out loud. I took a deep breath and confessed, "I'm lost, and I need some guidance." I took a glass to him. "Now get up and act normal before I send you back to your corner of the underworld."

He stood and took the glass from me. "Actually, my lord, my corner is quite nice, thank you."

I raised my eyebrows. "Don't you want to hear me?"

"Of course I do, my lord. That's not what …" He shook his head. "What can I help you with?"

"First, I don't want your help … I just need you to listen." As if listening would help me, let me vent. Like a therapist. So fucked up.

I asked him to sit down on one of the chaises, and then told him everything that had happened since he had been gone. I told him how Nadine felt guilty about killing him, that she had nightmares about him every night.

"She did the right thing," he said. "I don't blame her. If I could have, I would have asked her to kill me. There is nothing to forgive."

I opened my mouth to tell him I wouldn't say any of that to her but decided to keep going with my tale. I told him about visiting the Fates, the Cup of Life, Nasya, the tests, the Death Lords' betrayal. I told him I lost the cup, and the deal the Death Lords proposed.

I took off my shirt and showed him the black web spreading across my chest.

"By the Everlast," Morgan whispered. "Does it hurt?"

I shook my head. "Not anymore. It did, in the beginning. I guess it's a silent poison."

"But … what will happen when it—?"

"I don't know and that's not why I called you here. I just wanted someone to vent to."

He tilted his head, his eyes boring into mine. "Are you sure?" I remained quiet, and he continued, "Because you're a god, my lord. You don't actually need me or anyone else. You could summon a bunch of nobodies if you wanted just to be heard. But you called me."

I drank my whiskey in one swallow. At this rate, I wouldn't

be surprise if ninety percent of my body and soul were made of alcohol.

I groaned, hating how right he was. "Then, my newest advisor, what should I do?"

He cleared his throat. "Well, to put it bluntly, you should wipe that pout from your face and go back."

I sighed. "Easier said than done."

"Are you afraid of facing Nadine, my lord?" he asked. I averted my eyes. Was that so easy to see? He offered me a sympathetic smile. "Nadine doesn't know what happened with the Cup of Life, and she doesn't need to know. You don't need to give her false hope. Just keep going because nothing has changed."

"But it has."

"Not really, not to her." He stood and grabbed the empty glass from my hand. "Besides, they need you. They can use all the help they can get with this war. And you're not just any help. You're a powerful god." At the bar, he refilled our glasses. "Believe me, they will be glad to have you back. On their side."

He handed me my glass back. I stared at it, looking for answers as if they were hidden in the brown-gold liquid. If they had been, I would have found them by now, because I probably had drank enough whiskey to get a whole nation drunk. No, the answers weren't hidden in the whiskey. The answers were in Morgan. And in me too. I had already known what he would say, but hearing it out loud, hearing the truth from someone I trusted, seeing his serene and strong face while saying it, that was what I needed. That alone brought courage to my veins.

I pushed the glass aside. "All right. Let's get ready, then."

3

NADINE

My boots sank in the sand.

"Whoa," I said, staring at the sea.

Just three feet from me, the dark water glowed with millions of bright blue spots.

"Long ago, humans proved those shining spots were simply science," Victor said, standing beside me. "Phytoplanktons capable of bioluminescence. To a certain extent, they were right. But this was always Maho's doing."

"Whenever he stays a little while in a single location, the place absorbs his magic," Ceris added. "That's why many places believed in magic. Like the Ashikaga Flower Park in Japan, the Red Sea beach in China, the Zhangye Danxia Landform, also in China, and the Turquoise Ice in Russia."

"It's beautiful," I whispered.

"It was even more so before," Ceris said, her voice solemn as if she were mourning the loss of beauty, the loss of anything beautiful in this world.

Victor cleared his throat. "Let's keep going." He marched

on and Keisha followed. Ceris trailed after them, but I stayed for a moment longer. I had never seen a place like this before.

The waves rolled, creating white foam and bringing in more blue dots. I knelt down and sank my fingertips in the water. As if pulled by a magnet, the blue spots gathered around my fingers, dancing in an uncoordinated choreography. I moved my index finger to the side until it touched one of the dots.

"Ouch." I pulled back as a shock ran from my finger up my shoulder.

Energy. The blue dots were pure energy.

Magic.

"Nadine, are you coming?" The breeze carried Victor's voice.

I turned on my heels and sprinted to catch up with them.

We walked toward the center of the island for about five minutes while Victor and Ceris told us this place used to be an expensive vacation destination thirty years ago.

"The hotel on the other side of the island closed a decade or so ago, after the darkness spread," Ceris said.

The world changed a lot when the dark became permanent. Sometimes I wondered how there had been any order at all. Now, however, the world was spiraling down at a much faster rate. With Imha's attacks, everything had been thrown into chaos. The few world leaders who had survived the attacks were lost, not sure what to do or who to attack. Ceris told us about their theories: Russians attacking the United States, North Korea attacking South Korea and all neighboring countries, Cuba deciding to act. Secret organizations rising up to take over the world. Aliens. And more rarely, magic and even gods.

I guess the mind accepted a more rational answer before accepting the impossible ones, like magic and gods.

Our group discussed that topic from time to time. We wondered if Imha would reveal herself to the world, her powers and their creed, or if she would let the world assume it was something else entirely and retaliate against invisible threats. She had already let millions see her and Omi on several occasions. What went through the mind of the people who had seen her and survived?

My opinion was that, for now, Imha would let people think whatever they wanted. If the president of the United States wanted to believe all the attacks were terrorists or Russia, she would let them, because they would turn on each other and destroy themselves. But at some point, she would reveal herself—more than she already had. The few times I had seen her, that I had been in her presence, she gave me the impression she loved being stared at, being loved, and being worshiped. And that was exactly what she wanted. To be worshiped. By everyone who survived the end.

"Maho should be here." Ceris's voice broke through the haze of my mind, and I shook my head to clear my thoughts.

We were in a clearing among bushes and low, thin trees. White stones formed a circle with one crystal stone in the center. Ceris and Victor stood beside the crystal while Keisha walked the perimeter, her hand on the hilt of her sword.

Ceris pointed to the map. "This is where you saw his symbol, right?"

I took two steps to her and looked at the map in her hands. "I still see it." Maho's symbol, with its curled lines, was still strong and immobile in the exact spot we stood.

"Then where is he?" Victor asked, his tone curious, as if he wanted to solve a riddle.

"Do you see anything?" Ceris asked. "His symbol anywhere around here?"

I scanned the area. Dried grass, splotches of sand, bushes, and stones. Twelve white ones and one crystal one.

A crystal one.

I knelt in front of the crystal stone and squinted at it, as if there was something hidden inside. I leaned forward, placing my palm on it for support, and that was when the world spun.

"Whoa," Keisha cried, pulling her sword from its sheath.

The dark sky gained bright stars, the sand and grass became fog, and the stones glowed—the white ones shone white, but the crystal one radiated orange. Maho's color.

I stood, reaching for my weapon.

"I sense him now," Victor said.

"Me too." Ceris pointed somewhere amid the fog. "Right there."

All I saw was fog. "I don't see anything."

Keisha stood closer to the spot. "There's something here." She took three careful steps. "Yes, there's definitely something here."

Victor, Ceris, and I rushed to her side. With each step we took, the fog dissipated a little and we could see a shape forming in the distance.

A man with red-orange hair and freckles on his cheeks appeared amid the fog. He just stood there, the fog dancing around him, looking at us with big maple eyes. Like in my visions, he was dressed in an elegant white suit.

"By the Everlast," Ceris whispered.

"Maho!" Victor cried, reaching for him.

"Don't!" Maho shouted, his voice strained. He waved his hand to the ground. The fog opened up, revealing bright red chains around his ankles. "It's a trap. They've had me here for weeks, hoping you would come for me."

Victor narrowed his eyes. "They?"

"Edan and Nuri."

Those names didn't sound too unfamiliar. I thought hard about the books I read the past few weeks, trying to remember them, but nothing came up.

"Why?" Ceris asked.

"They want more than to live in Imha's shadows. They thought if they could steal my power, they would be stronger than her."

Victor's eyes bugged. "They have your power?"

Maho shook his head. "No, they don't know how." He lowered his voice before adding, "And I didn't tell them."

Ceris knelt in front of him and reached for the chains. She pulled back with a hiss as if they had burned her. "What kind of magic did they use?"

"Human blood," Maho said.

"By the Everlast," Ceris muttered.

"Never mind the chains," Maho said. "You have to go. Now."

Victor shook his head. "We won't leave you here."

"You must. When they realized they couldn't use my power, Edan and Nuri decided to use me as bait. They said you would come for me at some point."

"But ... they should be fighting with us," I said.

Maho tilted his head at me. "Who are you? Never mind. No time to explain. Just leave before they arrive. They will trap you too and use you. They will hand us all over to Imha and Omi."

"That doesn't make sense," Ceris said.

"Why?" Victor asked. "Why would they hand us to Imha and Omi?"

As if a fan had turned on above us, the fog pushed back, leaving us in a black hole. Keisha raised her sword and I pulled mine from where it hung at my waist.

"Because we want Imha and Omi to trust us." A woman with long, curly blond hair and a wicked smile stepped into the clearing from the shadows.

"And if she doesn't trust us enough to welcome us, we want her to at least leave us alone." A man appeared by her side. He had short blond curls and the same evil grin as the woman. They both had hazel eyes and wore similar black outfits like old military uniforms.

Edan and Nuri.

Now I remembered them.

Lesser gods under Sol—the god of the sun and day—they were a sick mix of siblings and lovers. If the tales were right, they weren't alone. I scanned the perimeter of the fog, identifying the shadows of several fire nymphs.

"Crap," I muttered.

"If you're not happy with Imha's and Omi's rule, why not fight them?" Victor asked.

The couple laughed.

Nuri tsked. "After she took down you and Mitrus, after all the chaos in the world, after all she accomplished, do you think there's a way to stop her?"

"We have to try," Ceris said.

"Try you might, but you will fail," Edan said. "And we prefer standing on the winning side."

"I can't believe I'm hearing this," Ceris said. "Don't you miss the world before Imha threw it out of balance? We can have that again if we fight her. We'll be stronger in numbers. Join us and fight her."

Edan sneered. "We already made our decision. Nothing you say will change our minds."

Ceris and Victor exchanged a look. They were getting ready to fight; I could feel it.

Nuri raised her hand and outstretched her palm. Fire licked her fingertips. "We sent a messenger to Imha and Omi some time ago. All we have to do is hold you until they get here."

The nymphs stepped out of the fog. Their long, flowy hair varied from yellow blond to red. Their skin was tanned, as if they spent too much time sunbathing, and their skimpy golden clothes did nothing to hide their lean bodies. Why were all deities so pretty?

The nymphs grinned at us and transformed. Their hair darkened, their skin went gray, their eyes became red, and their nails grew into claws.

"Demons?" I asked in a low voice.

"I'm not sure," Ceris answered equally low. "I just know they aren't themselves anymore."

The nymphs growled at us.

"Edan, Nuri." Victor stepped in front of Maho. "Think about what you're doing, please. There is another way." Behind his back, Victor pointed his fingertips at the chains around Maho's ankles. A thin strip of white power shot from his fingers.

"Trust the Everlast energy," Ceris said. She stepped back and did the same as Victor, though the power from her fingertips was pink. Together, the powers ate away the chains. "For millennia, we all trusted the Everlast energy. Why not trust it now?"

"Trust the Everlast energy." Nuri scoffed. "Where have you been the last thirty years? Have you seen what happened to the world? Where was the Everlast energy then?"

"The world was out of balance because of the goddess you're trying to make a deal with now," Victor said. He and Ceris were keeping our enemies occupied until Maho was free. "She threw the Everlast energy aside, but we can bring it back."

Edan shook his head. "I'm tired of waiting and hoping things will get back on track. A war is coming and we're choosing the winning side."

The chains snapped with a loud pop. Everyone froze.

Maho let out a long breath. "Right now, we're winning," he said, stepping to stand beside Ceris and Victor.

With a roar, Nuri lunged at Maho. Victor was ready and threw a white bolt at her. Edan engaged Ceris, and Keisha was surrounded by nymphs. Knowing I had more chances with the nymphs than with gods, lesser or not, I rushed to help her.

A nymph came at me and I jumped back, pulling my sword with me.

She was a nymph! I couldn't kill a nymph! What if we could change her back and she came to work with us?

Another nymph lunged at me, and I worked hard to parry and dodge without harming.

Ceris knelt a few feet from me and created a shield in front of her. "Nadine! They aren't themselves anymore." She looked at me, her stare quick but firm. "There's nothing you can do now to save them."

A swarm of nymphs rushed her. Ceris raised her shield as she threw bolts at them. A bolt hit the chest of the closest nymph. It exploded, opening a black hole in the nymph's chest. Her body fell on the ground with a thud, and then it crumbled into ashes.

I gulped, still retreating from the nymphs.

All right, Nadine. Focus! These nymphs are just like Morgan. They can't be saved. You need to kill them.

I took a deep breath and changed my stance.

Shutting down the part of my brain that told me I was again fighting innocents, I stopped playing and started attacking. I brandished my sword, eliminating as many enemies as I could. In less than five seconds, both nymphs were ashes around me.

More nymphs came at me and I fought on autopilot. Otherwise, I would think too much about what I was doing, who I was killing, and I would be sick. I would freeze again and I would end up dead.

I pulled my sword from the chest of a nymph and it fell on the ground. That was when I saw Edan and a half-dozen nymphs holding an injured Victor.

Nuri stood in front of him, holding a Black Thorn. "I wanted to wait for Imha and Omi to arrive, but seeing as you're not cooperating, I think she'll compensate us even if you're dead."

Nuri pulled back her arm, gaining momentum.

No!

Desperation gripped me. Victor couldn't die again. If he did, the war was lost. Even if his soul wasn't lost and he found a way to be reborn, it would take years for him to grow up and ready for battle again. There wouldn't be an Earth to fight for.

Something fierce, something strong surged inside me and I reacted. I lunged for the nymphs holding him, raising my arms to use my sword. A shock ran down my free arm and bright white light shot from my palm, sweeping over everyone in front of me. The light hit the nymphs, Edan, and Nuri, and flung them several feet away.

I froze.

Victor froze.

Ceris froze.

Keisha froze.

Everyone froze, watching me with agape mouths and wide eyes.

"What in the Everlast was that?" Ceris asked.

"Magic," Maho said, his voice low but sure. "Power just like ours."

"W-what?" I stared at my hand.

Victor stood. He walked to where Edan and Nuri had fallen. He nudged them with the tip of his boot.

"They are alive but unconscious." He looked at the nymphs around them. "The nymphs too."

The other nymphs, the ones I hadn't hit with whatever *that* had been, stood behind Keisha, looking confused. When Keisha, Victor, Ceris, and Maho turned to them, most of them fled. Only a brave few stayed and were quickly defeated.

Soon after, Victor teleported out with Keisha and Maho. Then Ceris, watching me with wary eyes, extended her hand to me. "Let's go home."

I gave her my right hand. She gripped it tightly and took us out of there.

4

NADINE

WE HAD TELEPORTED TO SEVERAL LOCATIONS BEFORE CROSSING the shield and suddenly appearing in the living room of the apartment in New York.

"So," Victor asked me as soon as I was aware of my bearings. "What was that?"

I shrugged, looking down at my hands again. "I-I have no idea." I still couldn't believe what I had done. It had to be a trick.

Ceris stepped back and glanced at Maho. "You said it was magic."

"It was," he affirmed. He was seated on the couch, his clothes disheveled and a bruise on his cheek. "I'm sure of it."

"Try doing it again." Ceris waved her hand and a target dummy appeared on the other side of the room.

I frowned at the dummy. "Try what? I'm not even sure what happened."

"Just do whatever you did," Victor said.

"I don't know what I did!"

"Just throw your hands up, aiming for the target," Ceris instructed.

"But—"

"Do it!"

Groaning, I positioned myself in front of the dummy. I wasn't sure what to do, but I was curious too—and frustrated. After all, I hadn't imagined that white light coming out of my hand. It really happened. Everyone had seen it.

I exhaled, trying to clear my mind of doubt or insecurity. I imagined the dummy was Omi, the god who murdered my family. Fury filled my veins. I focused on that, on that feeling, on how it enraged me, and how I could fight a thousand battles on it.

I threw out my hands.

Nothing happened.

I straightened myself, feeling pathetic. "I don't know what I'm supposed to do."

"The same thing you did when you saved Levi," Ceris said.

"I don't know what I did!" I yelled. Frustration welled up in me. Why were they bugging me?

Keisha cleared her throat and everyone looked at her. "Maybe it happened because she was in the heat of battle."

"Of course." Ceris nodded. "Seeing Levi being almost killed made her desperate. She just acted without thinking." I detected a hint of jealousy in her tone. She could calm down. I wasn't trying to save Victor for me. I was trying to save him for the world.

"Like, her emotions pulled the magic from wherever it's hidden," Keisha added.

"That makes sense," Maho said.

"If she had magic, would you be able to sense it?" Victor asked.

"Probably."

Ceris gestured for me to sit down beside him. "Let him sense you for magic."

"But ..."

She gripped my upper arm and pushed me to the couch. If she weren't a badass goddess, I would have shoved her away. However, I was curious.

Maho took my hands in his. "Relax and let me in."

What did that even mean?

He closed his eyes, and I felt it. A warm surge of energy seeped through my skin, traveling up my arms and reaching my heart. It was almost like the few times I had healed Victor, but instead of coming out of me, the energy came into me. Comforting and lulling. I bet if I let myself sleep now, I wouldn't have nightmares.

The energy traveled through my body, searching every inch of me for whatever it was looking for. Finally, it stopped in my heart and I gasped.

Maho withdrew his hands. "I can't sense anything."

"How is that possible?" Ceris asked, her tone irritated. "We all saw it. She used magic."

"Perhaps it wasn't hers. Perhaps she can redirect it?" he suggested.

"Could be," Victor muttered, eyes on me.

They all looked at me as if I were a lab rat. I felt naked and exposed. Worst of all, I felt like a failure.

The one millisecond I allowed myself to consider the fact that maybe I had magic, something like purpose filled me. Finally. Instead of being a human with a sword who could get hurt or killed, I could actually measure up to the rest of them and help.

But no. Whatever happened was a mystery, and it looked like it was going to stay that way.

I stood. "Instead of obsessing about things we can't control, how about we take care of Maho? He has been through a lot and needs some healing and rest."

"Right," Ceris said. Her posture rigid, she sat beside him.

While patching up Maho, Victor and Ceris asked him about his whereabouts for the last thirty years, how he had been caught by Edan and Nuri, and if he was willing to fight with us, to which he answered with a strong yes.

"Great." Victor smiled. "Welcome aboard, Maho."

After welcoming Maho to our little army, Keisha disappeared into the kitchen, saying something about making supper.

Maho then continued telling us about his adventures during the last thirty years. With Ceris's and Victor's attention elsewhere, I was able to slip out of the apartment and go for a walk around the building. I didn't know why I insisted on doing that. The outside looked and smelled terrible, with debris of the destroyed city littering the streets. Before we moved in, Ceris, Victor, and Micah had opened paths through the wreckage around the building and to and from the ward-slash-shield they had put up around the place, but it still looked terrible and gruesome. There were abandoned cars, purses, shoes, jackets, and trickles of blood everywhere.

I turned my head upward, looking at the dark sky.

Before finishing the Soul Oath with Micah, I wanted to see the sun for at least a minute. I had never thought about the night sky. Now a sudden despair hit me. I also wanted to see the moon and the stars. After we won the war, would he let me spend an entire day and night alive before finishing our deal? I hoped so. It would be fulfilling to see the sun, the moon, and the stars before dying.

I sighed. If we won the war.

If we didn't win, then it meant I died before being able to bring back my family and we all would be stuck in the underworld.

I sighed again and stopped forcing these crazy thoughts into my mind. They were better than facing the current problem, my current dilemma, because honestly, I had no idea what was going on.

I stared at my outstretched palms. "What the hell was that?" I asked myself.

It was something. We all knew that. We all saw when I shot magic out of my bare hands. But how had that happened and why? I had no idea.

A pang ran through my heart as I thought of Morgan and wished he were here. He knew so much about the creed. I bet he would know a book or two for us to look through, trying to match my abilities with someone from the creed. Or not. Why did I hope I would belong to the creed? It wasn't important. I would die in a few weeks, months at the most. It made no difference.

However, I couldn't shake the feeling there was more to it.

Holding on to a foreign hopeful feeling, I decided to head back to the apartment and search through the books Ceris had brought when we moved—and pretend Morgan was by my side, helping me.

———

After taking a refreshing shower and grabbing

something to eat, I went to the dining room, which had become our meeting room.

I read through the spines of the many books around the place, grabbed a few that looked promising, spread them over the table—careful not to knock over the scented candle burning in the center—took a seat, and started to read.

The titles of the books varied from *The Everlasting Circle Mythology* to *The Dictionary of The Everlast Creatures*. Even though I hoped to find answers here, I knew it was a long shot. At least it gave me something to occupy my mind other than playing what happened repeatedly in my head, thinking about Micah, and checking the map for new deities every five seconds.

"Hey."

After almost an hour alone and in silence, the new voice startled me. I looked up from the book I was skimming through and saw Keisha standing at the room's entrance. "Hi."

She glanced at all the books on the table. "What are you doing?"

I leaned back in my chair and shrugged. "Passing the time."

She took two steps inside the room. "By?"

I sighed. "Researching. Trying to see if I can find something about what I can do. Or what I should be able to do." I pressed my fingertips to my temples and rubbed in circles. "I don't know what I'm doing anymore."

She took a seat across from me. "I can help."

I offered her a weak smile. "Thanks, but even I'm not sure what I'm looking for."

"It's okay. I can help anyway." She pulled one of the books to her and flipped it open. "I'll just do the same thing you're doing. Look for someone with or something about your abilities."

My abilities. Weren't abilities things we could control? I couldn't freaking control anything!

The shuffling of pages was the only sound for several minutes.

Until Keisha started, "So ... how are you?"

I raised my gaze to her and scoffed. "Is that supposed to be funny?"

She crossed her arms over a book and leaned forward, holding my gaze. "No. How are you?"

I sighed again. It seemed my current life required a lot of sighing.

Why was I still so guarded with Keisha? She had already proved she was a good friend. I could open up to her, I knew that, but every time I thought about confiding in her, insecurity stopped me.

But here she was, willing and friendly, goading the answers out of me.

"I'm ... not too good, I guess," I confessed.

She nodded. "A lot has happened in the last few months. It's understandable."

A whole lot I still had no idea how to deal with. And it hurt each time I stopped and thought about it. That was why I did this. That was why I trained nonstop or found things like researching to occupy my mind. Otherwise I would break down and I wasn't sure I could get back up this time.

"How about you?" I asked, trying to be nicer to her.

One corner of her lips tugged up. "I'm okay. I mean, I'm doing fine, but all of this is hard. We win one day, and lose another day, and ... well, it's war. I know I'm a hero and fighting is my thing, but I want peace, you know."

I nodded. "Me too."

"I want peace too," said a new voice. Keisha and I looked at Ceris, standing like a Greek statue under the archway that separated the dining room from the living room. She held a tray with three mugs. "Sorry, I didn't mean to sneak in. I just saw you two and I came to ask what you're doing."

Keisha and I exchanged a look. The first thought that crossed my mind was to tell Ceris it was nothing and hope she moved on. But something nagged in my chest. She had been somewhat nice to me the last few weeks—or less horrible—and even though she would never be Cheryl to me again, it would be nice to not bicker with her all the time. That started by actually reaching out, which was what she was doing now. Now it was my turn to reach out and tell her the truth. Plus, judging by the smell, she had brought coffee with her.

"Researching," I said. "Trying to find anything about my freakish abilities in these books."

Ceris scanned the room and the piles of books. "I'm not sure there's any book here that will answer that, but we can certainly try." She sat down at the head of the table, between Keisha and me, put the tray on the table, and passed each of us a steaming mug.

"Thanks," I said, taking mine. I closed my hands around it and rejoiced in the warmth seeping into my hands. I inhaled deeply, loving the smell.

"Thank you, my lady," Keisha said with a head nod.

Ceris pulled a book from the center of the table and opened it, seeming interested in our research.

I skimmed through three books and found nothing that matched my abilities.

"Oh my God." I pushed the book aside and lowered my

head on the table, welcoming the coolness of the smooth wood against the skin of my forehead. "The Everlasting Circle is huge. Too many deities, nymphs, and demons ... so many different kinds and sizes and colors. It's too much. I'll never find it."

Ceris snorted.

I lifted my head, watching her with wide eyes. Did the goddess of beauty just snort?

"What?" Ceris asked. "Can't I be amused that after only a couple of hours of research, you're giving up?"

I rolled my eyes. "I'm not giving up. I'm just commenting how hopeless this is."

"We'll find something," Keisha said, picking up a new book from the pile and pushing it across the table toward me. "If you keep going."

I groaned, but I picked up the damned book. Before I opened it though, I turned to Ceris. "You went out yesterday to look for more allies, right?"

"Yes," she answered, her eyes on the book she was flipping through.

"How is that going? How many allies do we have so far?"

The goddess lifted her eyes to me. "Not enough." I thought she wouldn't say anything else. She was our leader in this endeavor, and she could simply not want to share anything with me. Then she surprised me. "We need to find Sol, Lua, and Ronen. As much as I'm glad that I've found lesser gods and other deities, we need the power of the gods and goddesses of the Everlasting Circle to win this war."

Keisha agreed as I said, "I've checked the map twice since we returned from Maho's island, but what the hell." I extended my hand to her. "I can check again."

With a pretty wave of her hand, Ceris produced the map

out of thin air and passed it to me. I unrolled the yellowed paper and leaned over it. The symbols danced and swirled and twirled around the map, but no other god's or goddess's symbols were fixed in one point.

"No one else so far," I said, rolling up the map.

Ceris sighed. "We will find them. We have to."

5

___

MICAH

Rok flew in circles above my head as I stood outside the protective shield, rethinking my plan. What was wrong with me? I had nothing to rethink. Ceris, Levi, and Izaera knew where I had gone, and they expected me to come back. What they didn't know was how long I would be gone. I hadn't known either.

But I was here now. I was back.

I wished Morgan had come with me. I couldn't simply restore him to life, but I could trade his soul for a new one. He refused, of course.

"I won't let you kill an innocent to free me," he had said.

I had told him I wouldn't kill an innocent. I would just time it for when Imha killed an innocent. I would use his or her soul in exchange for Morgan's. Still, he had refused.

"It won't feel right," he had said.

After all the crap we had been through, he chose now to do the right thing.

I took a long breath and stepped through the shield. I weaved through debris and abandoned cars for a few blocks before I reached the building. By now, the other gods would have sensed me. They would know I was coming.

It is about time, Levi's voice invaded my mind.

I didn't answer. I honestly still didn't know what I would tell them about the two weeks I had searched for the Death Lords, and then the week I had been holed up in that shitty motel, feeling sorry for myself.

I signaled Rok, and he let out a sharp squawk before flying away. I opened the building's front door, went up the stairs—I glanced at the spot where I had kissed Nadine before I left—and halted in front of the closed apartment door. I took another deep breath and reached for the knob.

The door flew open before I could even touch it.

"What took you so long?" Ceris asked, her eyes accusing, her tone harsh.

"Let him in," Levi said from somewhere behind her.

With a grunt, Ceris stepped aside and I entered the apartment. Instantly, I looked toward the gym room, expecting to see Nadine sparing with Keisha, but no one was there.

Energy hit me, and I realized there was a new deity here. "Maho," I said, but I didn't see him. "Maho is here."

"He's in the back room, resting," Levi said. He was standing by the window, looking at the "beautiful" view outside.

I stood my ground in the middle of the living room and crossed my arms. "How did you find him?"

Standing behind the couch that was placed between Levi and me, Ceris tsked. "You answer our questions first. What took you so long?"

I looked around. Nadine wasn't in the living room, the dining room, or the kitchen. I could sense her aura if I wanted to, but I avoided doing that. It felt like invading her privacy, and if she knew, she would hate me more.

I sighed, letting my arms droop down beside me. "I failed."

I told them everything. About the island, Nasya, the Cup of Life, and the Death Lords. I also told them I had been searching for the Death Lords all this time, but I didn't tell them about the deal with the Death Lords. I didn't tell them about the black tendrils of poison spidering across my chest, and I certainly didn't tell them about the Black Thorn in my pocket.

Levi leaned against the windowsill. "You knew it was a long shot."

Yes, I did. But I was also hopeful, especially after passing Nasya's tests.

"I'm sorry," Ceris said.

I stared at her. Wow. Her tone, her expression. She actually meant it. "Me too," I admitted.

"What are you going to do now?" Levi asked.

I shrugged. "What we were doing before. Find allies, fight Imha and Omi. What else can I do?" I frowned. "I don't feel Izaera and Zelen."

"They have been out, looking for allies," Ceris said.

"And Maho?"

"Nadine found him," Levi said.

That was a nice surprise. "What? How?"

"She had the idea to use the map to find them, the same way she found our scepters," Levi explained. His tone held a hint of pride. "She has only found Maho so far, but we're hopeful she'll pinpoint all the gods and lesser gods."

"That would be a great help."

Levi nodded. "It would."

"That's not all," Ceris said. "Yesterday, when we arrived on the island in Thailand to get Maho, Edan and Nuri were there. They had Maho imprisoned. We fought them, but they managed to pin down Levi. Nuri had a Black Thorn."

Fuck. I looked over at Levi. He seemed well, though. "And?"

"Nadine saved me." Levi smiled. "Again."

"Wait. How?"

"She used magic," Ceris said.

I gaped. "Magic?"

"Yes. She lunged at Nuri and it looked like she was going to use her sword, but then magic shot from her hand. She knocked them all out. Literally. Edan and Nuri and the nymphs were all unconscious after her magic hit them."

"So ... she has powers?"

That was certainly an unexpected development. A good unexpected development. With magic, Nadine would be able to defend herself better during battles—which always worried me. Half of my mind was always on her, concerned she would get seriously injured during a fight. I tried not to worry because I knew it pissed her off, but when I could, I butted in and saved the day. It was my way to ensure she would be okay.

Ceris tsked. "Well, apparently she doesn't. Maho couldn't sense any power in her after we came back."

"He suggested she redirected power from us somehow," Levi said.

I frowned. "I didn't even know that was possible."

"We're not sure it is, but whatever it was, it was powerful."

"What was powerful?" Nadine's voice echoed from the hallway. She stopped by the archway and my breath caught. She wore jeans and a tank top that hugged her perfect body.

She had a hand towel around her shoulders, and she ran her fingers through her long, wet hair. Barefoot, she looked casual and relaxed—until her gaze found mine. Her face paled and her beautiful green eyes went wide.

Fuck. I thought I had been prepared to see her again, but the force of the longing that rippled through me almost brought me to my knees. It was all I could do not to run to her, take her in my arms, inhale her delicious scent, and hold her close.

I cleared my throat. "Levi and Ceris were telling me what happened when you all were rescuing Maho."

She nodded and averted her eyes. Without another word or glance in my direction, she marched to the kitchen.

"Her mood hasn't been the best," Ceris said once Nadine had closed the kitchen's door. I nodded, knowing all too well I was partly responsible for her bad mood. "I'll go talk to her."

Ceris joined Nadine in the kitchen and I exhaled. This wouldn't be easy.

"I'm really sorry about the Cup of Life," Levi said. "I wish there was something I could do to help."

I snorted. If only he knew. "Unless you know where the Death Lords are hiding, there's nothing anyone could do."

A knot creased Levi's forehead. "Wait. What if we found them?"

"I've been trying for the last three weeks."

"I know, I know, but two heads are better than one. Perhaps you didn't look for them in the right place."

"And where could they be?"

"I don't know, but I'll brainstorm." He took a step forward and clasped my shoulder with a strong grip. "I don't want to feed you false hope, but I don't want to see you give up yet."

I wasn't sure I could handle more crushed hope, but there

was nothing else in the world I would like more. Even the war and the restoration of the balance seemed like trivial things when compared to losing Nadine.

Because I would lose her. Even if she died and went to the underworld and I summoned her like I had done to Morgan, she wouldn't be the same. She would be dead, trapped in my underworld, and Nadine deserved more than that. She deserved to live, to smile and laugh, to sing, to see the sun rising and setting.

I closed that part of my mind and heart before hope took hold of me. I couldn't let myself hope. Not anymore.

With every ounce of strength I had, I said, "We have more important things to take care of."

6

NADINE

CERIS SAT ON THE OTHER SIDE OF THE KITCHEN ISLAND, looking at me as if I was going to burst into flames at any second. Here was the only place in the apartment where Ceris hadn't lit scented candles—probably because it already smelled of coffee and whatever else we were baking or cooking.

"What?" I asked her again.

"Nothing," she answered again.

I wasn't buying it. I reached for one of the sandwiches Keisha had made for dinner and left on a tray for us. Ceris took one too.

"Why are you babysitting me?"

"I'm not babysitting you."

"Yes, you are." I took a long drink of water. The cold drink washed down my throat, reinvigorating me. She thought I was going to let my emotions get the best of me—the emotions I was desperately trying to ignore. Oh my God, Micah was here! He was back! He had even spoken to me. He had stared at me. And I honestly didn't know what to make of that. She thought I was going to explode on Micah, demanding he … what? I had no right to demand anything from him. I sighed. "Look, I won't do anything stupid, okay?"

"What if I want you to do something stupid?" She took a bite out of her sandwich.

"W-what?"

She lifted a finger, asking me to wait while she finished chewing. After she swallowed, she said, "Well, you shot magic out of your hands when your emotions were high during a battle. Maybe being irritated with Mitrus and getting into a fight with him will trigger another response."

I gaped at her. "You can't be serious."

"Why not? It seems like a good test."

"You're crazy." I ate the last bite of my sandwich, grabbed my water, and marched out of the kitchen. I braced myself, expecting to see—and ignore—Micah again, but he wasn't there. Neither was Victor.

Disappointment took hold of me and I gasped, startled by the emotions swirling in me. I shouldn't feel disappointed. I should feel relieved.

Afraid of my own feelings, I rushed to my bedroom. It was too early to sleep though, so I immersed myself in the books spread across the floor. I had brought a few from the dining room the other night so I could read them in bed, but my mind wouldn't cooperate. It kept drifting to the man—to the god—somewhere in this apartment.

In the past, Micah had pushed me away on certain occasions, and on others he had cornered me and wouldn't leave me alone. We had kissed, then he left without any explanation, and he stayed away for three weeks.

Now he was back and I didn't know what to make of it, of us, of him … of anything. Should I confront him like an abandoned girlfriend? Should I ignore him? Should I treat him like a regular friend or acquaintance? Or should I treat him like a god? Call him my lord and bow to him every time I was forced to speak to him?

I shut the book on my lap and let it slide to the floor. Why bother reading if I wasn't actually paying attention to the words on the pages?

Perhaps it was too early, but I was exhausted. I was still tired from yesterday. Between the traveling, fighting, and the inexplicable magic, I felt drained. The shower and the sandwich had helped, but I really needed some peace and quiet. I hoped my body and mind were so tired I wouldn't have any nightmares. It would be a first.

I changed my tank and jeans for a loose tee and sweatpants and slipped under the covers. I hugged Pinky, my little sister's stuffed bunny, and closed my eyes, willing my thoughts to good things, which seemed like a hard task. In the world we lived in, nothing was good anymore. The only good things I could think of had been taken from me.

My family had been killed right in front of my eyes. My father, my mother, my little sister, and my two little brothers. And many years before that, my other brother had died. Then, a few weeks ago, I had killed Morgan.

How could I find any peace?

I rolled in my bed, thinking of a time when my family was alive, when we were happy together. I thought of my last birthday, when Micah took me to see them in the underworld. That brought a small smile to my lips.

Micah would never admit it, but he had a soft spot. Taking me to see my family, even if I couldn't interact with them, had been the best present anyone could have given me. I wished he would take me there again. But I still hadn't decided on a course of action—ignore him or treat him like an acquaintance—so that was out of the question.

Finally, my mind relaxed and I could feel the edge of sleep coming to take me.

The weirdest dream invaded my mind.

"Come on, I will show you," a girl said. *She smiled and her bright eyes twinkled. Her dark hair was pulled back into an intricate braid with white flowers woven into it. Her smile, her face ... I had seen it before. "I think you'll like him."*

I took a moment to situate myself. We stood behind some rocks on a hill, watching over a village on the vale. A village with houses made of poor wood and straw. Women dressed in simple gowns walked around with baskets full of clothes or bread. Men sported odd pants and shirts, thick belts and boots—and bows on their backs and daggers at their waists. The children played around them, most of them barefoot on the unpaved and uneven ground.

I looked at the girl beside me. She wore an elegant white dress, much like the ones Greek goddesses wore in modern depictions. Looking down at me, I noticed I wore the exact same dress, and my hair was pulled back in the exact same fashion.

"There he is." She pointed to a man exiting one of the houses. Like the other men, he had a bow and quiver filled with arrows on his back and a dagger tucked in his belt. "Isn't he handsome?" She sighed.

Yes, he was handsome. Not like Micah and Victor, but those two were gods. They were abnormally perfect. This man, the one this girl was showing me, was handsome in a natural and casual way.

"I know this is dangerous. I know I shouldn't, but please try to understand." Her eyes pleading, she grabbed my hand.

Like the script of a play had been downloaded into my brain, I finally understood what was happening in this crazy dream. This girl was my sister, my twin sister, my best friend. We weren't supposed to be here, but she was in love with the man in the village and he was in love with her.

I was happy for her, but I also feared where this would lead. She wasn't supposed to fall in love, not with someone like him. Not with a mortal.

The man stopped at the corner of a house on the east edge of the village, looked around, and then rushed up the hill.

"Come on," the girl said, squeezing my hand. "He'll be waiting for me."

She set out running and my body jerked with her pull. I fell into step with her. Disbelief burned in my veins.

I took a long breath to calm down, then another. Then a third one, but this time it wasn't to remain calm. It was to help me breathe easier. My vision blurred, and my legs wobbled. The burn spread, searing white hot in my limbs.

I fell on my knees.

"What is it?" the girl asked, kneeling in front of me.

My vision darkened and the pain exploded. I heard her calling me, but then she was gone.

I sat up on my bed, screaming my head off as the pain burned in my chest.

My bedroom door flew open and everyone in the apartment hovered over me.

"Nadine, what's happening?" Ceris asked.

"What is it?" Keisha asked.

"Say something, darling." That was Micah.

I closed my mouth and swallowed my scream. I would have snapped at him for calling me that, but I was afraid if I opened my mouth, I would only scream more.

I lay down again, fighting to breathe through the pain while everyone talked and asked questions at the same time.

Their voices, their agitation, only made it worse. I gasped, taking in a lungful of air, but it came in hitches, hurting more than helping.

Would this pain, this burn ever go away? What if it didn't? Maybe this pain was here to claim me, to take me. I didn't want to die yet. I had to remain alive to fulfill the Soul Oath and bring my family back to life. If I died now, it all would have been in vain.

"Nadine, what is going on?" Ceris asked, her voice close. "Tell me what you're feeling."

I tried, but I couldn't. I opened my mouth to tell her, but only whimpers came out.

She placed her hand on my chest and warmth seeped in, warmth much different from the burning in my body, warmth made of love, of life. After a few minutes, I was able to breathe again. The pain was still there, burning like a bitch, but at least I didn't scream each time I opened my mouth.

"You healed me?" I croaked. It hurt to speak.

"Not really," she said. "Healing isn't one of my powers, but I passed good vibes on to you, hoping to dull the pain."

"Are you still hurting?" Victor asked.

I nodded.

"What happened?" Micah asked. His eyes shone with concern. Or maybe it was something else. I was probably too tired and hurt to see anything clearly.

"I ... I don't know." I took a deep breath. "I was having an odd dream. The pain started in the dream, and I woke up burning on the inside."

"What dream?" Ceris asked.

"I don't know. It was ... odd. I was ... it was a long time ago, like centuries ago, and I had a sister. A twin. She wanted to show me something, someone, but before we could get wherever she was taking me, the pain started. And I woke up."

"With the pain," Micah said.

I nodded, not looking at him. "With the pain."

"How is it now?" Victor asked.

I closed my eyes and assessed it. "Still here, still burning, but I can breathe and speak through it now."

Micah turned to Victor and Ceris. "Do we have something for this? A medicine, a potion?"

"I'm afraid without knowing what exactly is afflicting her, we could risk doing more harm," Ceris said.

With gentle hands, Maho touched two fingers to my forehead and closed his eyes, breathing deeply.

Moments later, his eyes snapped open and he looked down at me. "The pain is magical."

"W-what?"

"Magical pain?" Victor asked, staring at me as if I were a lab rat again.

Micah crossed his arms. "What do you mean?"

"It's not physical pain," Maho said. "There's nothing wrong with her. It's pure magic."

"So now there's magic in her?"

He nodded. "Yes, but it's not hers."

What did that even mean?

"Is there anything we can do for that?" Micah asked, his eyes hard on Maho.

The red-haired man shook his head. "Not right now. Maybe a healer could lessen the pain."

"Do you know where to find a healer?" Micah asked Ceris.

"No, but I can search for one," she said, her tone indicating she didn't really want to go.

"It's okay," I said, closing my eyes. "It's slowly diminishing. I just want to rest now."

Even with my eyes closed, I could feel their gazes on me. And I heard whispering. They were talking, planning in hushed tones.

"Someone should stay with her," Micah said, his voice low.

"I'll do it," Keisha said. Thank God. If Micah had proposed to stay, I would have screamed some more. "I'll stay here with her."

Keisha exited the bedroom with the others. When I opened my eyes, Micah stood under the doorjamb, looking at me with worry in his eyes. With a grunt, I rolled on my side and gave him my back.

"Excuse me, my lord," Keisha said.

I spied over my shoulder as Micah retreated from the bedroom and Keisha entered with a sleeping bag. She closed the door behind him and then sat by my bed.

"You don't need to stay," I said. "I'm sure I would scream again if it got worse."

She chuckled, though it wasn't an amused tone. "I know, but I want to."

"Why?"

She lifted one shoulder. "It just feels right."

I passed my pillow to her. "At least try to get some rest too."

She smiled. "Will do."

I tucked my hands under my head and closed my eyes. Hopefully, the pain would lessen and I would be able to sleep —nightmare or crazy dreams free.

7

MICAH

I couldn't sleep knowing Nadine was in pain a wall away. I would have volunteered to stay in her bedroom, but I didn't think she would let me, so I didn't argue when Keisha offered. At least someone would keep an eye on her.

First, she had used magic, then the inexplicable pain. What in the Everlast was happening to her?

There was someone who knew more than he should about the creed.

I exited the bedroom, trying not to make any noise so I wouldn't wake up Maho. I stopped in the living room to pick up the leather jacket I had left draped over an armchair, and exited the apartment. I sprinted down the stairs, out the building, and through the cluttered streets until I was out of the protective magical shield. Sensing my presence, Rok flew from behind a dead tree to me. He landed on my outstretched hand and I petted his black feathers.

"You know what to do," I said. I could swear he nodded before flying away again.

I teleported to my lair and summoned Morgan.

He looked confused for a second before realizing where he was. His eyes settled on my face and a frown followed. "Is there something wrong, my lord?"

I plopped down on the chaise lounge. "It's Nadine. Something is happening to her."

The frown deepened. "What?"

I told him what I knew about the magic and her pain.

"She was still in pain when I left," I told him. "According to Maho, maybe only a healer can ease her pain. Maybe."

"Has Ceris found any of the creed's healers yet? To join the cause, I mean?"

I shook my head, feeling helpless. "No. Deity healers aren't easy to come by."

Morgan sat down on the chaise beside mine and stared at a wall. "That's ... so weird."

"That Ceris hasn't found any healers yet?"

"No, no." Morgan stared at me. "About Nadine."

"You know almost everything about our creed." There was a reason Ceris had sent Nadine and Levi and me to find Morgan a few months ago. He was the high priest that knew the most about our creed. "Can you think of anything that relates to what's happening to her?"

He chuckled. "I hardly know everything, my lord. You're the one who has been living for many millennia."

"Unfortunately, the millennia all blur together after a while. And many things are easily forgotten. So, can you think of anything?"

Morgan stayed quiet for a minute, a knot between his brows as he stared at the floor, deep in thought. "No, my lord, not really. What makes you assume whatever is happening is related to the creed?"

"I don't know. Everything so far has. She's far more connected to all of this than we all realize, I'm sure of it."

He nodded. "I think so too."

"From what Ceris told me, they have been researching Nadine's abilities but have found nothing so far."

I laid down on the chaise and stared at the crystal chandelier hanging from the high ceiling. Where could I find more information? I raked my brain, trying to remember high priests throughout the centuries who had had too much access to our creed, or places that could hold more knowledge about us.

Nothing came to mind.

Just like when I had lost the Cup of Life to the Death Lords, I felt useless, hopeless. I fucking hated this feeling.

Morgan went to the bar and prepared drinks for us. It was way too early for whiskey, but who cared? When Morgan offered me a glass, I didn't think twice. I downed the contents of the glass in a single gulp. The amber liquid burned my throat, and I liked how it didn't treat me well. I didn't deserve to be treated well. Not now, not ever.

"Don't worry," Morgan said, taking the empty glass from me. "We'll think of something, my lord."

8

NADINE

I DIDN'T THINK IT WAS POSSIBLE, BUT I WOKE UP BEFORE Keisha. Trying not to make any loud noises, I tiptoed out of my bedroom and went to the bathroom where I brushed my teeth and changed from my pajamas to working out clothes —black pants and black tank top. Because I was in the mood for black. Or was it because black matched my mood?

As I walked to the kitchen, I saw Ceris, Victor, Maho, and Micah in the dining room, having what looked like an important meeting. A tiny pang sliced through my chest. They were having a meeting without Keisha and me. It was okay, I told myself, and I entered the kitchen. They were all mighty gods. They were supposed to have ultra-secret meetings.

I found fresh coffee, prepared two slices of toast, and sat down at the kitchen island. I tried focusing on each bite and sip I took; instead, my mind went to the dream and the pain from last night. I shuddered. What a crazy thing.

A crazy thing, which maybe could help with my research. It was one, or two, more items we could look for—crazy dreams and magical pain. I snorted. Yeah, right, because that would be easy to find.

I went to the sink and washed my plate, then poured more coffee in my mug. I usually avoided looking out the window, but a shadow caught my eye and I saw Rok flying by. I followed him with my eyes and observed as he landed on the broken window of the building across the street. He squawked once, and I could swear the raven was looking at me.

"Hello to you too," I whispered, remembering how Micah had asked it to keep an eye on me before. God, it had been only a couple of months ago, but it felt like years had gone by.

Turning around, I leaned back on the counter and smelled the delicious scent of pure black coffee. I hadn't had a mochaccino since Ceris took Victor from Cathedral Rock, and honestly, I didn't miss it. One more point to confirm my theory I had never actually loved him, not for real.

Not like I loved someone else inside this apartment.

I sighed.

The devil walked in the kitchen.

Micah looked gorgeous, as always. A little longer, his hair was even messier than before, but the new style suited him. The strands framed his face, accentuating the sharp lines— his chiseled jaw and chin, as well as his high cheekbones. His black eyes shone like two dark pools, and his lips ... I sighed. His lips had a permanent pout, as if they wanted to be kissed. His black T-shirt hugged his broad shoulders and ripped arms, and his dark jeans were fitted around his legs and hips. Before this craziness of gods and demons and magic, I would have said—to Raisa or Olivia or even Cheryl—that he had been sculpted by the gods. Ha! How ignorant of me since he was a goddamn god!

"Morning," Micah said, his eyes meeting mine.

Realizing I had been staring, I lowered my gaze to my coffee. "Morning."

He grabbed a mug from a cabinet and came to my side, where the coffee machine was. "No more dreams or pain?" he asked as he poured coffee in his mug.

"Nope."

"Good." He turned around and his elbow brushed my arm.

A cold shock ran up my arm and an image flashed in my mind.

In what looked like those old taverns from old movies, the young girl from my dream—my sister—stood several feet in front of me. She leaned over the wooden bar counter, talking to the barmaid who was cleaning glasses. The handsome man we had seen before came over to her side and leaned his back on the counter. At first, he stood there, looking out at the crowd taking up the tables at the tavern. Then, slowly, he turned around, his elbow brushing her arm, and she looked at him, and he looked at her. Time froze. They stared at each other, a smile forming on their lips as if no one else existed in the world.

I gasped as the image faded.

Micah turned to me, his body looming over me. "What it is?"

I shook my head, clearing the fog from my mind. "I ... I just saw the girl from my dream again. A quick scene, but it felt like ... a memory." A knot appeared between his brows and his black eyes stared at me with concern. I couldn't take it. I averted my eyes. "I don't understand."

"And the pain?" he asked, his voice low and firm as if he was ready for battle.

I took a step to the side, needing more space from his powerful figure. "No pain this time."

Micah took a deep breath, puffing out his chest and growing taller—making me feel smaller, weaker, and unimportant—and leaned against the counter. "You should start taking notes of these dreams," he suggested. "Perhaps we can make sense of them together." I glanced at him. "All of us," he added quickly. "Ceris and Levi are good with these things." He cleared his throat. "You're sure you're okay? No pain?"

"I'm okay," I said, my voice low, faint.

Micah nodded. "Good." He sipped from his mug, and then turned his body toward me. "I ..." Anticipation took hold of me and I held my breath. A long, tense moment passed before he simply pursed his lips and shook his head once. "That's good."

With hooded eyes, Micah nodded again. Then, without another word or glance back, he walked out of the kitchen.

That was it? After all the weeks he had been gone, after kissing me and leaving, that was all he was going to say to me? He wasn't even going to apologize for being a jerk?

I let out a long breath, as if now that he was gone I could breathe easier. But that wasn't true. It was hard to admit, even to myself, but I felt safer when he was around. Yes, I felt small and weak when beside him, when confronting him, but that was only because he was so tall, broad, and powerful. Otherwise, he had been a safe harbor through it all—except when he was leaving me behind. I missed the way we were before, when we talked more, when we helped each other, when he still needed me to heal him. Now that he was a full god, he didn't need me anymore. Who needed a simple mortal?

I turned to the sink and washed my mug, wishing it were

that simple. If only I could wash all my problems and frustrations away.

———

I didn't let go of the map anymore. I kept searching it, looking for any symbol that might stop long enough for us to go after it. Two days passed and I must have checked the map at least a hundred times between training with Keisha and avoiding Micah.

Finally, on the morning of the third day, I found one.

"Here," I said, my tone chipper. "This is ..." I looked at the book for the right symbol. "This is Sol, god of the sun and day."

Ceris leaned over the couch where I was seated to look at it. "That looks like a place he would hide."

"Isn't Lua with him?" Maho asked. He was seated in an armchair across the room.

"No," I said, looking at the book to check on Lua's symbol. Then I went back to the map. "Her symbol is all over. It doesn't stop for long."

"That's okay. At least we can reach Sol," Ceris said. "He might know where Lua is and then we'll have another one on our side."

"Great," Victor said. "Let's get ready, and this time we'll be more careful."

Thirty minutes later, we were in our armor, carrying our weapons, and popping in and out of places so our energy would be harder to follow. One of these spots was the edge of a lake from where we could see a village on the other side. A village that was under attack. People ran around, screaming and crying, fire engulfed houses, and demons swept through the place, killing everyone who crossed their paths.

"Wait," I yelled before Ceris could take us out of there. "The village. We have to help them."

Ceris gave me a hard look. "We can't help everyone."

I glared at her. "But we have to try. Isn't that what we're trying to do? Save the world? This is part of the world. Demons are attacking innocent people. We have to help."

Micah stood beside me, towering over me. "We'll help them." He unsheathed his sword and turned his back to us, marching toward the village.

Victor followed Micah. "Let's go."

Ceris groaned and I stifled a grin.

We rushed around the edge of the lake and charged into the village.

Adrenaline shot through me. Fighting was dangerous and messy and bloody, but it was also exhilarating. It could be beautiful in a deadly way, with the long, precise movements and twists and jumps.

"Nadine, Keisha," Victor called out. "Help the people. Get them out of the village. We'll take care of the demons." He opened his arms and white bolts sparkled to life in his palms.

The women and children yelped at the sight, but when he walked by them and threw the bolts at the demons, they sighed in relief.

"This way," I shouted, gesturing to the edge of the lake.

Demons followed us, but Keisha and I were prepared. We used our swords to defend the townspeople, killing the demons after a few blows. A few men joined in the battle with their personal guns and some even carried kitchen knives. My mind wanted to take a moment and ponder the dangers of having untrained men handling guns, but there was no time. If they could help us, even if it was by distracting the demons, I would take it.

A few yards from me, Micah jumped from a bench, sending a black energy wave out from his body. It hit several demons in their chests. The demons flew back and Micah advanced on them, a determined shine in his dark eyes. The way he danced around the innocents and struck the demons was mesmerizing.

It hit me once more how out of my league he was. He was a god—they all were gods—and I was a mere mortal who tried to bargain her way into helping. I had no idea why they put up with me. Why they just didn't leave me behind, abandoned me in a safe town and be done with me. I was glad they hadn't, though. I couldn't bear the thought of waiting for this war to end and doing nothing. Especially now that my family was gone. If the creed left me, I would be truly alone.

Most of the people from this side of town seemed to have made it to the lake.

"We should go to the other side," I told Keisha.

She sliced the throat of a demon before nodding.

As we turned to leave, a young woman came running in our direction. Her blond curls were mated with blood, as were her sweater and jeans. She screamed as demons trudged behind her.

Keisha and I acted. We ran to the girl, our swords raised to stop the demons. In less than twenty seconds, Keisha and I had killed them all.

I turned to the girl. "Are you okay?"

She stood there, her wide eyes shifting between the demons at our feet and the swords in our hands.

"Hey," Keisha called. "Are you okay?"

The girl blinked and tears filled her eyes. "Y-yes." Then

she shook her head. "No. They killed my family." A sob shook her body.

My heart squeezed. I knew all too well how it was to lose your loved ones.

She raised her hands and hid behind her palms as another sob raked through her. Two gashes on her lower arm trickled blood down to her elbow—probably from demons' claws.

"You should have that looked at." I pointed at her arm. She peeked through her hands and followed my finger.

"Oh," she said, lowering her hands. "I hadn't even noticed it."

I reached for her, cupping her wound. I just wanted to make sure it wasn't too deep. Just as I touched her, a shock ran through us and she jumped back.

Her mouth closed, her eyes hardened, her slumped shoulders straightened.

"I need a weapon," she said.

"W-what?" Keisha asked.

The girl looked around. A few feet from us, a gun lay beside a dead body. The girl picked it up, opened the magazine, and checked for bullets, and then she snapped it close again.

"Only eight rounds," she said. "Better make them count."

She raised her arms and pointed the gun at the demons. Her eight bullets hit four demons—in the heart and in the head. The demons fell to the ground.

Keisha and I stared at each other.

"I need another weapon," the girl said, flinging the gun aside as if it was a used piece of paper. Her eyes locked on Keisha's waist, where a spare one-hand sword dangled. "Give me that."

Keisha didn't move.

A demon rushed to us. In our stupor, the girl stole my sword from my hands and twirled around, raising the sword and slicing the demon's head off.

She whirled the sword and handed it back to me by the hilt. "Here. Now, if you could please give me that one." She pointed to the extra sword at Keisha's waist.

Keisha looked at me, unsure what to do. Stunned, I nodded and Keisha handed the sword to the girl.

Her blue eyes sparkled as her hands closed around the hilt. "Let's kick some demon ass." She let out a loud battle cry and charged the demons, fighting like Keisha and me, fighting like she had done it her entire life. "What are you two waiting for?" she yelled.

I shook the shock from my body and joined her in battle.

9

MICAH

WE WEREN'T SURE WHO WAS BEHIND THIS FREAKY BATTLE, BUT there were demons everywhere.

Nadine and Keisha, and now that blond girl, were doing a good job of escorting the people out of town, and Ceris, Levi, Maho, and I were doing a great job dispatching the demons.

"Can you sense anyone else?" I asked Maho as I threw a bolt at a demon. The bolt exploded on its chest and the demon exploded with it.

"No." Maho played tricks with his magic. He created images of himself and taunted the demons, then took them out effortlessly. It was kind of fun to watch.

"But there has to be someone," I muttered. "They wouldn't just attack a town by themselves."

"Perhaps they were sent here," Ceris said as she rushed past Maho and me. "Imha is decimating every city and place she can reach. Maybe she's dispatching the demons without a commander."

It could be, but that still didn't make much sense.

The horde of demons was diminishing. We would be done with this hiccup in our mission soon.

Like lightning, Rok appeared from nowhere and flew to me, squawking like a mad bird. That could mean only one thing ...

Fancy meeting you here, Amiel's voice rang in my head.

Shock froze me.

You're behind this attack, I asked, scanning the area. He had to be close.

Actually, no. We've just followed you here. It's easy to find you when we're all so deeply connected.

This damned connection—that now was one-sided. When I became a full god again, I noticed I couldn't sense them anymore. But apparently, they could still sense me.

I groaned as I withdrew my sword and engaged a demon. I needed to burn the pent-up rage swelling in me right now.

What do you want? I asked. Rok flew in circles over my head, making me even more enraged.

The same thing as before, Amiel stated. *We have the Cup of Life and you have a beautiful opportunity to have Levi killed. I bet you can even make it look like the demons got him.*

I snorted. As if demons could simply kill a god. Well, they could, but it was difficult to accomplish.

"Go," I muttered to Rok. "Go find them."

The bird stopped with his nonsense flying and dove away, going for the hills behind the houses.

I see your new pet, Amiel said. *She's beautiful.* I pierced my sword into a demon's chest and let out a furious roar. *I see now why you want to save her. I would want that too and—*

Don't you dare come near her.

I wouldn't dare, my lord. His words dripped with sarcasm. *Not while you're alive anyway.*

With a voracious cry, I swung my sword wide and cut off the head of a demon.

"Whoa," Maho said, staring at me with wide eyes. "Everything okay over there?"

"Everything is perfect," I snapped.

If you ever touch her—

If you kill Levi and take the Cup of Life, you won't ever have to worry about that.

The Cup of Life.

I faltered in my step and a demon swiped his claws at my shoulder. With renewed rage, I drew a bolt in my palm and buried it deep inside its chest. The demon was gone in less than a second.

Can you imagine eternity with her by your side?

Of course I could. I dreamed about it every day.

But killing Levi … I couldn't do that.

I looked over my shoulder at where Levi fought with several demons. He was a good fighter. He would never go down easy. It would be hard to make it look like an accident.

I shook my head. What the hell was I thinking? I couldn't kill Levi.

Your window is ending. Soon the demons will be gone. And so will we … with the Cup of Life.

Several yards behind Levi, Nadine was fighting alongside Keisha and the blond girl. Even now, seeing her all badass and kicking the demons' butts, I wanted to protect her, to help her, to keep her safe. If she received one little scratch, I would lose my shit.

What would happen when she lost her life?

A pain I didn't want to acknowledge spread through my chest. I couldn't lose her. I just … couldn't.

I took out the two demons rushing toward me, then

turned to Levi and moved closer. I shut down the logical part of my brain as I used magic to trip Levi at the same time a demon made a swipe at him. Levi fell on his knees and the demon's claws almost ripped through his enchanted armor. Bewildered, Levi tried to get to his feet, but I used magic again to force him down on all fours. Six demons had surrounded him and grabbed hold of him.

Levi jerked against them, trying to push them away. He would have made it, if I hadn't used magic once more to increase the pressure the demons were exerting over him.

Levi's eyes widened as he looked at the face of a demon that was raising his claws, ready to swipe deep and nice. His eyes looked past the demon, right at me.

"Mitrus," he rasped. "Help!"

But I didn't move. I couldn't move.

The swipe wouldn't kill him. I would have to do it.

"Levi!" Ceris voice boomed behind me. She ran past me. "What are you doing? Help!"

She lunged at the demons.

And I snapped out of it.

Shame filled me as I released the magical hold I had on Levi and charged the demons. Levi, Ceris, and I killed them all.

Then both of them turned to me, the expression on their faces livid.

"What the hell was that?" Ceris yelled, her voice shaking the ground underneath us.

I ran a hand through my hair, sighing. Wishing I had an answer for her.

Inside my head, Amiel tsked. *So close.*

Go fuck yourself.

He laughed, the sound echoing in my skull, making me sick.

———

M*ICAH*

A*FTER SAVING THAT LITTLE TOWN, WE PROCEEDED WITH OUR* mission to find Sol.

We were on high alert, expecting to find more demons or lesser gods or some other deity. And I had been tense, expecting Amiel and the other Death Lords to keep following me. Nothing had been simple so far, why would this be?

But it seemed they were gone since Rok, who was in charge of finding and following the Death Lords—unsuccessfully—came back to me not long after.

The only thing we found was a few weak wards and a half-assed hidden Sol. Once he saw us, he dropped the wards and came with us, no questions asked, except to query about Lua.

"We thought maybe you would know," Levi said.

"I haven't seen her in years," Sol said, his voice dejected. "We had a fight many years ago and still haven't made peace."

Which didn't make sense. They were soulmates. They were supposed to be together, to help each other, to support each other, to never leave each other's side.

Ceris and Levi, on the other hand, bombarded me with questions once we were back in the apartment.

"What the hell was that?" Ceris turned to me, right in the middle of the living room with everyone watching. "You saw demons pinning Levi down and you just stood there. You didn't help him!"

"I did help," I said. Not a total lie, but my help had only come after she had come to his aid.

Guilt and shame mingled in my chest. The pull to glance at Nadine, to see the expression on her face as she witnessed this accusation against me, was too alluring, too enticing. But I resisted it.

"You stared at me, Mitrus," Levi said, his voice laced with disappointment and fury. "They had me and you did nothing."

I opened my mouth to yell some lame excuse, but Maho talked before I could. "I don't understand. How were they able to pin you down, brother?"

"I ... I don't know," Levi said.

"Perhaps Mitrus's theory that there were more than demons hiding out there was right," Maho said. He had no idea how right he was.

"Perhaps." Levi's blue-green eyes bore into mine and I could see, I could feel, how troubled he was.

I sighed. I felt troubled too.

How could I have done that? How could I have held him down and let the demons have at him? I wasn't the same Mitrus as before. I wasn't evil, not like Imha or Omi. I ... I wished we could go back in time. Instead of actually listening to Amiel, I would have alerted the others to his presence, and we would have hunted them down. We would have wiped them from this Earth.

That was the right thing to do.

I swallowed my pride and said, "I don't know what happened. If you say I should have acted sooner, then I should have. I'm sorry."

Ceris's eyes widened, and Levi actually looked taken aback.

After several tense seconds, Levi cleared his throat. "Okay."

He faced Nadine, Keisha, and the blond girl. Then, I dared a glance at Nadine. She was watching me, a pretty knot between her pretty green eyes. She held my stare for five seconds—I counted—and then looked at the new girl too.

"What's your name?" Ceris asked the newcomer.

"Alice," the girl said, her voice clear and firm.

"Alice," Ceris repeated. "I should tell you that, like our Keisha here, you are a hero. Welcome to the Everlasting Circle."

10

———

NADINE

ALICE AND KEISHA FOUGHT WITHOUT WEAPONS WHILE I WAITED my turn. I observed them, taking note of things they could have done better or moves they had missed.

Alice had come with us after we found Sol. When Ceris told her who she was, what the Everlasting Circle was, and who they all were, Alice took everything like a champ. It was like she had been waiting for this to happen. She didn't question anything—at least she didn't voice any doubts out loud.

The only part that hurt came right after Ceris made proper introductions. Alice turned to me and asked, "But what are you, Nadine?"

The golden question.

I shook my head and walked into the kitchen while Ceris explained how I had helped them and about my newfound abilities.

To make matters worse, I had another dream about the young woman. She, my twin sister, and I needed to hide something, something big and powerful, something that emanated with power, but each time I tried to look at it, it vanished as if by magic. Although I knew it could have been only the dream. My dreams were always dubious, with things disappearing and floating around. To hide this mysterious object, my twin and I pulled daggers with the hilts encrusted with precious gems from our waistbands near our backs, and we didn't even flinch as we slashed our palms open. Blood oozed from the new cuts and dripped on a large rock atop of a hill. The rock shone bright, and then the thing was gone. Fire exploded from the trees around the hill, and I could hear my family's screams, accusing me of killing them. I woke up breathing hard and trembling from head to toe as the intense pain slithered through my chest. But I pressed my lips tightly and swallowed my screams. I didn't want anyone coming to babysit me.

The next morning, Alice was already in the gym when Keisha and I entered in the early morning.

We started with stretching, followed by a little bit of cardio and weight lifting, and then we went on to fighting practice.

So far, Alice could hold her own against Keisha.

Then it was my turn with Alice. We started by circling each other, taking in our space and our reactions. Alice feigned a few times, trying to trick me. But I didn't fall for anything. When she actually came at me, I was prepared. I met her move for move, until she used her superior strength to her advantage. As tall as Keisha but as lean as me, Alice surprised me by hitting like a truck. The girl could pack a punch!

I twisted at the last second, and instead of hitting my chin, her fist connected with my shoulder, throwing me off balance. I stumbled two steps, but recovered, ready to plant a roundhouse kick to her chest.

Then two of our scouts walked by the door and I let my guard down.

"What happened?" Alice asked.

"The scouts are here," I said, already walking toward the door.

Keisha and Alice followed me to the living room where Ceris, Victor, Maho, Sol, and Micah waited for the scouts' report. Rok was seated on the windowsill, watching everything with interest.

"As expected, things are getting worse and worse," the blond scout said. I knew he was some deity Ceris had found, but I didn't remember his name, or what he was and what exactly he was doing for us. "Per Imha's orders, several of her demon battalions are supposed to go from town to town and destroy everything and kill everyone."

"Which explains what we encountered yesterday," Ceris said.

"Our spy told us Imha is doing that because she knows you won't stand for it and will try to help as many people as you can, which will, in turn, deviate from your plan of assembling an army to attack her."

"I see," Ceris said, her voice strained.

"Also," the tall one with brown hair started. "She knows you're after the other gods, Lua and Ronen, and apparently that's her main mission right now. To get to them before you do."

"She mentioned killing them if they don't join her cause," the blond scout said.

Ceris glanced at me, a sense of urgency in her blue eyes. I sighed, knowing that finding Ronen and Lua depended solely on me. No pressure.

"All right," Levi said. "Thanks for the update. You should

keep doing the same. Monitoring Imha's and Omi's moves. See if your spy can find out anything more about what they plan next, other than finding Ronen and Lua."

"Unfortunately, our spy isn't too high ranked in her army, my lord," the tall scout said. "So he might not be able to find out anything more interesting."

"That's okay," Levi said. "Anything he can tell us is of great help. Thank you."

Both scouts bowed and then hurried from the apartment.

Before I could move or even think, Ceris turned to me, the map in her hand. "You know what to do."

With a sigh, I grabbed the map and plopped down on the couch to search for the goddesses.

11

MICAH

I was a bundle of nerves, of irritation, of rage, ready to explode. The night before, I had dreamed of Nadine. Actually, it had been a fucking nightmare. I didn't remember all the details, but in my dream, I had the Cup of Life in my hands and Nadine had agreed to drink from it. She had agreed to spend eternity by my side. Then I lost the Cup of Life again, and Nadine blamed me for it. She blamed me for her impending death, the death of her family, and Morgan's death. She cried, she raged, she punched me. And there was nothing I could do because I agreed with her. She was right. I had been an asshole, and it was my fault. The last thing I remembered was the Soul Oath coming to fruition, and Nadine dying in my arms. Even in death she hated me.

"I'll never forgive you," were her last words.

I woke up wanting to punch the wall. The first thing I had done that morning was to go for a run, to see if I could burn off some of my frustration. But I had barely begun when the scouts arrived.

As they spoke to Ceris and Levi, an idea popped into my mind.

I still had a chance to recover the Cup of Life from the Death Lords, as long as I could find them.

As soon as the scouts left, everyone dispersed. Nadine looked for Lua and Ronen on the map while Maho stayed by her side, studying her—he was still intrigued by all the magic around her and all that she could do. Ceris and Levi and Sol discussed the next plan on their agenda. Keisha and Alice went back to training.

And I quietly left the apartment and went after the scouts. Rok followed me, and I felt his accusing eyes on me, as if he knew what I wanted and disapproved of it.

"Your fault," I told him. "If you had done your job, the only job I asked of you, I wouldn't have to do this."

The raven squawked and flew away as if I had hurt his feelings.

I caught the scouts a few feet from the ward.

"My lord," Rihan said, bowing his head.

I stood tall and controlled my voice to sound firm, authoritarian. "I have a new order. One of you needs to search for Amiel, Jed, Keon, and Riel."

"The Death Lords?" Letos asked. "Do you have any idea where we might find them, my lord?"

I nodded. "They have been following me. They must be close by."

"I can do it," Rihan said, turning to Letos. "Ask Tuzin to cover for me while I'm gone."

"Will do," Letos said.

They both bowed to me again, and then stepped through the ward around the building.

Even with a half-assed plan in motion, the pent-up irritation was killing me. I needed more than a run around the block. But what?

Not sure what to do, I marched into the apartment and saw Nadine training with Alice and Keisha.

My breath caught.

She was a beauty, and she moved with lethal charm. Despite everything, she had become an expert warrior and rivaled the heroes—not an easy feat for a mortal.

Pain sliced through my chest again and I groaned. Mortal. Yes, she was mortal. And right now, there was nothing I could do about that.

But there was something I could do about the rage and irritation brewing inside me.

12

NADINE

AFTER THE SCOUTS WERE GONE, I SEARCHED THE MAP FOR A while but didn't find anything. When Ceris noticed nothing was happening, she let me go, and Alice and I resumed our fighting practice.

We were at each other for over five minutes, matching punch by punch, kick by kick, and always dodging, always parrying. Neither of us could get a good hit.

I was about to duck and swipe my feet under her, which was sure to give me an advantage, when she lowered her guard and pivoted to the door.

"My lord," Alice and Keisha said in unison. They bowed low as Micah strolled into our improvised gym.

With a bored look, he waved his hand at them. "Girls, could you please step out and give Nadine and me a minute?"

My eyes widened as the girls hurried out of the room, and Micah finally looked at me.

I folded my arms. "What do you want?"

For a moment, he didn't speak. He just stared at me, his black eyes wreaking havoc in my soul. It was hard not to notice how beautiful he was, especially when I was mad at him.

His long and broad figure looked too damn hot in black pants and a thermal tee and boots.

I sighed.

"Always on the defensive, darling." His serious expression broke into his trademark naughty grin, and I fought the urge to roll my eyes at him.

"What do you want?" I repeated.

He lost the grin and those black eyes turned too serious again. "To train with you."

"I have Keisha, and now Alice, to train with me. I'm good."

He shook his head. "They are a good pair for physical fight training. But what about magic?"

"What about magic?"

"We'll be dealing with deities who will first use magic as their main weapon. You gotta learn how to fight them."

I swallowed. "You know I only used magic once, and I have no idea how to replicate that."

He took a step closer. I wanted to retreat, but I held my ground, unwilling to show him how much his presence, his closeness impacted me. "I'm not asking you to use magic. You'll fight with what you have." He gestured to the weapons lining the wall.

"I don't get it."

"I'll fight with magic, and you'll use a sword."

"How fair is that?"

One corner of his lips tugged up. "Exactly. That's what you'll encounter on the battlefield, and it's not fair. You should be prepared for it."

It made sense, of course, but I wasn't about to tell him that. I preferred being on the defensive.

"And why aren't you offering to train Keisha and Alice too?"

The smirk on his lips spread a little more. "Because you're special, darling, and you deserve special treatment."

What the hell? That angered me, but instead of confronting him, I decided to be the bigger person and walk away before things got out of hand. I took three steps toward the door and froze before the fourth step when a black bolt zoomed past me, missing me by a few inches, and hit the wall behind me.

I gaped at Micah. "Are you crazy?"

He produced black flames over his open palm. "You have no idea."

I stared at him, shocked by his behavior. Knowing he wouldn't really hurt me—I hoped—I walked on. Until two bolts crossed my paths, one right after another.

"What ...?" I shut my mouth. I wouldn't dignify this by actually talking to him.

"Fight!" he urged, his black eyes shining. He conjured another bolt of black flames. "Come on, darling. I know you want to get a hit or two on me. Fight!" He threw the bolt, and this time if I hadn't jumped back, it would have hit me.

I was past words. Rage tore through me and I rushed him. His wicked smile widened as he shifted his weight, ready to attack. Two bolts appeared in his hands. But a couple of feet from him, I detoured to the side, crouched down, rolled on my back, and shot up by the weapons wall. I grabbed a wooden training sword as a black bolt flew at me. I side-stepped, and it exploded on the wall, rattling the weapons.

I took a short dagger from the wall and threw it at him just as he was conjuring another bolt. That made him stop and move, letting go of the bolt.

"Nice," he said, his tone amused.

In the meantime, I took other daggers from the wall, hoping to use them soon.

Then Micah was on me again, throwing black balls of energy, one after another. I was able to run from a couple, and I parried a few with my sword. When they touched the metal of the blade, they exploded, rattling the sword and my arms. The first time I did that, I almost fell on my butt, but as I parried bolt after bolt, I grew used to their strength and matched it with mine.

It was hard to get to him when he was throwing his magic at me nonstop. And that was what the daggers were for. I threw one at him, forcing him to twist his shoulders to avoid being hit, which gave me enough time to race three steps to him before he could throw another bolt.

I lifted the sword over my head and yelled as I was about to strike. Micah cast a shield in the middle of the ten inches that separated us. My sword slammed into the shield and bounced back, rattling my arms and shoulders, and sending me sprawling on my back.

"Ow," I muttered.

Before I could recover, Micah stood over me, one foot on each side of my hips, a wicked grin on his lips, and a black bolt in his hands.

He winked. "I win, darling."

Renewed rage ripped through me. I pushed my knees to my chest and curled my hips up, freeing my legs from his. I opened my legs and swiped at him, but Micah was ready. He jumped up, and then fell on me, his knees stranding my hips and his feet on my knees.

I scanned the room and saw my sword on the floor by my side. I reached out, but it was still a few inches away from me.

With his powers, Micah flicked the sword and it skittered away.

"What the hell?" I screamed.

He leaned over me, aligning his face with mine. He stared at me, the intensity of his gaze too much for words. My breath caught. For a moment, I lost myself in the depths of his black eyes, dreaming of other moments we shared like this. Moments that had given me hope that ... that he liked me more than he let on. That he liked me almost as much as I loved him.

His hand shot up and his fingertips grazed my skin as he brushed a strand of hair that had come loose from my pony-tail. His touch sent rivulets of want, of need into me, and I shivered.

Then his lips were mere inches from mine, and I found myself arching my back, reaching up to him.

"Like I said, darling. I win," he said.

The spell shattered.

With a scream, I threw my hands up, intent on pushing against his chest and getting him off me. Instead, white light shone from my palms and white bolts flew up, hitting Micah's chest and flinging him five feet in the air and all the way across the room. He hit the wall with a loud grunt. The bolts faded and he fell on his knees. I sat up, gaping at my hands. What had happened?

A cough broke my shock and I shot up, rushing to Micah as he struggled to stand. Dread and panic rose in my chest. Had I hurt him?

"Micah! Are you okay?" I went to grab his shoulders, but he started laughing. Really laughing. I froze and stared.

"That was ... incredible," he said, his voice a little hoarse.

I flinched, taking a step back. He kept laughing and I

slapped his shoulder. "You scared me! I thought I had really hurt you!"

With a loud sigh, Micah's laughter died and he looked at me, a smile on his lips. "I'm okay, darling."

I slapped his shoulder again. "Stop calling me that."

"Stop hitting me," he said, but his tone was still light and teasing. "Good practice, don't you think?"

I frowned at him. "Did you do this on purpose? To get me to use magic again?"

He shook his head. "Not really. My intention was to prepare you for what's to come. And to spend some time alone with you. But I'm glad it happened. Now we know it's not a fluke."

"How do you know? I could still have channeled it from you."

"I was paying attention, darling. I didn't feel anything. You didn't use my powers. You used yours."

I raised my arm to slap him again, because I was still mad at him—for pushing me to do this and for letting me think I had hurt him—but then he closed his hand around my wrist and pivoted, pressing me against the wall with his body.

"I'm proud of you, darling," he whispered in a husky voice.

His hard body against mine, his gruff voice, his sandalwood scent ... it was too much for me. I couldn't think straight. I knew I should be mad at him, that I should push away from him, but I didn't have the strength to do it. I didn't have the will. I wanted him right where he was.

Micah shifted, aligning his hips with mine, and I felt how aroused he was. I gasped.

"I'm always proud of you." His breath danced over my lips and I leaned into him, needing to have more.

Voices and footsteps boomed from the apartment.

Micah jumped three feet away from me, and with my weak knees, I had to lean against the wall not to fall on my face.

Victor and Ceris burst into the gym first.

"What happened?" Ceris asked, looking from Micah to me. "We heard crashes and screams."

With a serious, somber expression, Micah turned to them. "We were training." He glanced at me and his eyes were already different. The intense and amused shine was gone, replaced by something I couldn't quite grasp. Was it pain? Frustration? Sadness? It didn't make sense. "Nadine was able to use her magic again."

"What?" Victor said. He smiled at me. "That's great."

"No," I said, finally pushing through all the emotions causing turmoil inside me. "It's not great, because I didn't do it on purpose. I still don't know how to control it, how to call it."

"But you did it," Ceris said. "That must mean you weren't channeling our magic."

"I was paying attention," Micah said. "She didn't draw it from me, and I'm guessing you all were too far for her to draw from you."

"That's ... good news," Victor said. "I think. If you keep practicing, you'll be able to do it again."

I picked up the wooden sword from the floor. "Perhaps we should research more before actually letting me use it. We don't know what kind of magic it is, or what I can do with it."

I thought about the panic I felt when I saw Micah flying across the room. I would have killed myself if I had hurt him. I didn't want to feel that despair ever again.

"I understand your apprehension, but we've been

researching for days now and have found nothing. We shouldn't let this momentum get away," Ceris said. "We can start with small spells, things that are sure not to hurt anyone. Meanwhile, we keep researching."

Looking at Ceris, Micah said, "I'll leave you to it, then."

Once more, Micah simply left. No second glances, no explanation, nothing. He just upped and left.

And I berated my stupid self for deep down hoping that one of these days he would actually stay.

13

NADINE

THIS TIME, WHEN THE DREAM STARTED I KNEW EXACTLY WHO I was in it and what was happening.

Inside what looked like a small, bare bedroom, the young woman halted in front of me, her eyes filled with tears. "You have to understand. I love him. I can't live without him. I need to stay with him."

The actions and words took me over, as if I had rehearsed them a long time ago. I retreated a few steps from her and stared at her as if I didn't know her at all.

Dread surged in my chest. "What did you do?" I asked. She put a hand over her mouth to stifle a sob. Her silence was enough. "No, you didn't. No, please, tell me you didn't."

Slowly, she dropped her hand and met my eyes. "I did," she whispered. "I'm sorry. I knew you wouldn't understand if I asked for your help. So I did it alone."

I shook my head as panic replaced the dread in me. "Oh my gods."

She reached for my hand. "We'll still be sisters and friends. Forever."

I took another step back. "No. Not forever." Anger and betrayal edged my panic and I welcomed them. "I can't believe you did this. Do you have any idea of the consequences? Of course, you don't. Otherwise, you wouldn't have done it."

"I know the consequences." She wiped her tears. "I chose him over whatever may happen."

"May happen? It will happen!"

I stormed out of the bedroom and the world spun in darkness. I blinked and the dark dissipated. I was back in the volcano, and in front of me, Morgan stood with his hand on his stomach, blood seeping between his fingers.

"You killed me," he said, his voice laced with shock and disgust.

"Oh, God," I whispered, reaching for him. "I didn't."

"You killed me!" he screamed.

I halted. "Please, forgive me."

"I knew you were evil. I knew you would ruin us all."

Tears brimmed in my eyes. "No, no."

"You, Nadine, will be the end of our world."

I sat up in my bed, breathing hard. My hand jumped to my racing heart and I was glad this time there was no pain with the nightmare.

What the hell was that? First the crazy dream, then the nightmare with Morgan? What was next? A nightmare about the murder of my family? There was only so much I could take.

I lay back down, but my mind and body were too agitated to quiet down. At least there wasn't any crazy pain today. Reluctantly, I scooted out of my bed and tiptoed to the kitchen. I closed the door to make sure I wouldn't wake anyone, and grabbed a tub of chocolate chip cookie dough ice cream from the fridge. I had no idea how Ceris still found ice cream and soda and several other luxury items in our decaying world—and right now I didn't care.

I picked a spoon from the silverware drawer and sat on a stool on the kitchen island. I probably should serve a scoop or two in a bowl, but I was too agitated to care. I dug in the ice cream tub, knowing I should control myself before I ended up eating everything.

Of course, my mind wandered to the odd dream and the nightmare. I didn't pay much attention to the dream, but I hung onto the nightmare. God, poor Morgan. He had been one of our most resourceful assets and a good friend before the Crimson Dagger did a number on him—and I had killed him.

A lump rose in my throat. When would this guilt leave me? Never. I knew that. And I kind of didn't want it to leave me. If I felt guiltless, it meant I didn't care about him, and I did care. I would always care.

In need of something to wash down the lump clogging my throat, I stood and snatched a soda from the fridge. When I closed the fridge door, I jumped back.

"Oh my God, you want to give me a heart attack?"

As he leaned against the counter beside the fridge, Micah's serious eyes set on mine. "Can't sleep?"

I shrugged and returned to my stool and ice cream. I popped the can open and drank a long swallow. The lump was still there.

With a beer in hand, Micah sat on the stool across the island. "What was it this time? Pain or nightmare?" I didn't answer. I didn't even look at him. I just stuffed more ice cream into my mouth. He sighed. "Look, I get it, okay. I was a jerk today during practice, but I swear to you that wasn't my intention. I would never hurt you, not int—"

"Don't," I snarled, looking into his eyes. "Don't say anything. I don't want to hear any excuses."

His jaw set. "Fine. But you know we'll be around each other all day, every day, right? You can't ignore me forever."

"I can try."

"What else do you want me to do, Nadine? Want me to kneel in front of you and beg for forgiveness?"

Even if I said that was exactly what I wanted, would he know what he was asking forgiveness for? I doubted it.

This was going nowhere. Like he said, we would be around each other every day. If I kept up this effort of ignoring him, I would become grumpy and my usefulness would dwindle further. Time to drop the hormonal teenager act and behave like a responsible adult—the war and its effort came before any boy-girl drama.

I dropped my spoon and shoved the ice cream tub aside. "There's nothing to forgive," I said, though deep inside I wanted him to tell me he was sorry for pulling me to him then pushing me away. For kissing me then leaving without explanation. For acting like a lust-crazed lunatic this afternoon, provoking me, and then shutting me down again. "We don't need to be best friends to fight a war together." I took a sip of my soda. "It's all fine." One eyebrow raised, he tilted his head to the side, as if trying to figure out my logic. I didn't give him a chance. "What are *you* doing out of bed?"

He lifted one of his shoulders. "I heard noises and came to check it out."

The shield around the building didn't let anyone inside, and if someone got in, the gods would be able to sense it way before they got inside the apartment. He knew that. "Well, it could only be me, or Keisha or Alice, or one of the gods. No need to come check it out."

"I wanted to." The gleam in his eyes darkened, too intense. I averted my gaze. "Before I came back, I was in the underworld," he said. That caught my attention and I glanced back at him. "I checked on your family. They are doing well." I held my breath, not expecting this. I let out the air in my lungs slowly, relieved my family was okay. "I also checked on Morgan. Actually, I spoke to him."

My heart stuttered. "W-what?"

"When he died, the charm from the dagger released him. He's the same Morgan as before."

That was ... that was good to know. However, it made me feel worse. I had killed him. I had killed our good friend, one of our best allies.

Tears brimmed in my eyes. "And?"

"He's fine." Micah reached across the island and took one of my hands in his much larger one. "He knows you did what you had to do. He understands. He knows he had to be stopped. He said to thank you for ... ending him."

I opened my mouth, but nothing came out. Morgan *thanked* me for killing him? Who in the hell did that?

"But ... I killed him. How can he thank me for that?"

"I told you, he understands. He said he would have done the same thing if the roles were reversed."

I gulped. So, Morgan would have killed me if I had been the one affected by the Crimson Dagger. I understood. If I was that out of control and there was no cure, I would have wanted someone to stop me. Still, didn't make it any easier to accept the fact that *I* had *killed* him.

I stared at Micah's hand on mine. Why was he so nice and caring sometimes? I wished he would decide what he wanted. The cocky, self-centered Micah who flirted with all the girls and kept me at five arms' lengths, or the one that looked at me in a way that took my breath away.

I sighed. It didn't matter. It would never matter. Not with the ticking clock over my head.

I pulled my hand free from Micah's. "Thank you," I whispered. "For telling me this."

"You're welcome."

———

"I FOUND RONEN!" I ANNOUNCED FROM THE LIVING ROOM. Everyone else was in the kitchen, cleaning up after lunch. I had eaten with them, but then something itched in my mind and I had to look at the map instead of lingering in the kitchen and talking while washing the dishes and putting everything away.

Ceris and Victor were the first to run out of the kitchen and sit beside me on the couch. Micah was the last one, and he lingered by the door, his arms crossed, watching us.

"Where?" Ceris asked, leaning over the unrolled map on the coffee table.

"Here." I pointed to a small town outside Moscow where the symbol of the goddess of entertainment had shown up, bright and strong.

Ceris frowned. "Why would she be there?"

"It doesn't matter why," Victor said. "All that matters is we should go get her."

"Now?" Keisha asked. She stood in the middle of the living room, her pose ready to strike, even though she didn't have any weapons with her. Well, she didn't need any to inflict serious damage.

Victor stood from the couch. "Yes, now. Let's gear up and meet back here in fifteen minutes."

Everyone scrambled out of the living room and went to their rooms to get ready. Alone in my bedroom, I shrugged out of my workout clothes, which had become like my daily uniform, and started putting on my gear—beige suede pants with patches of intricate leather on the sides, a fitted white thermal tee, a leather vest with the same intricate pattern, a belt to hold our weapons, and beige combat boots.

I was pulling the tee over my head when a soft knock resounded on my door. Before I could answer, it opened and Micah peered inside.

"Oh," he said as his eyes fixed on my exposed midriff.

I quickly yanked the tee down. "What is it?" I snapped, crossing my arms over my chest as if I could erase what he had seen.

Clearing his throat, Micah stepped in my room. "I was coming to see if you needed any help."

"With what?"

He shrugged and gazed at me. Heavy tension hung around us as we stared to each other, both with our defenses on high alert.

After what seemed an eternity, Micah grabbed the beige leather vest from my bed and approached me. I made to take it from him, but he kept it out of my reach.

"Just let me do this," he said, his voice devoid of any sarcasm or teasing. It was tiring really, never knowing which Micah I would get. In the end, the almost begging shine in his black eyes won me over and I nodded.

Like I was a five-year-old child, Micah helped me put my arms through the sleeves of the vest, tugged it tightly around me, and pulled the zipper up. When he was done, he didn't retreat his hand from the zipper, but he lifted his gaze to meet mine again. He was so close that I was able to hear the sharp, muted breath he took.

Then he grabbed the belt from my bed and placed it around me. "Now you're all set."

I narrowed my eyes at him. "What are you doing?"

He stepped back but straightened his back and stuffed his chest, as if protecting himself from what was to come. "Helping you."

"You know that's not what I meant. I'm not a child. I can dress myself." I raised my chin high in defiance. "What are you doing?"

He lifted one shoulder. "I don't ..." He pressed his lips in a tight line. "I—"

"Let's go, people," Victor called from the living room.

"We should go," Micah said, hurrying out of my bedroom as if it were on fire.

Sighing, I knelt down and put on my boots, before taking the sword and the dagger from my bed and sheathing them on my belt.

I didn't even want to think about what had just happened and what it meant and why Micah could possibly be acting this strange, because if I did, I wouldn't focus on the task and would be screwed.

Like an army battalion, we marched from the building to the other side of the wards where the gods offered their hands to Keisha, Alice, and me so we could teleport with them. I started reaching for Ceris's hand, which was closest to me, when Micah's heavy hand closed around my shoulder.

"I've got you," he whispered.

Before I could protest, the earth was yanked out from

under my feet and the world revolved around me. After three quick stops, we were all standing in a dark alley.

As soon as I confirmed we were in the right place, I jerked away from Micah's touch and wrinkled my nose. The place reeked of rotting food, waste, and other putrid odors.

Ceris peeked around the corner of the alley. "I can sense her," she said, looking side to side. "It's clear."

In groups of twos or threes, we exited the alley and walked along the unpaved streets of the small town. The buildings weren't tall and they looked uncared for. Broken windows, peeling paint, and dying gardens. There were a few houses here and there, and they all looked abandoned. To be honest, the entire place looked deserted.

As the last group, Micah, Keisha, and I were on high alert, looking over our shoulders and even at the buildings and houses, cautious of prying eyes and surprise attacks.

"Can you feel her?" I asked Micah.

He shifted his eyes from a dead garden to me. "Yes. She's close."

I nodded, looking down at my feet.

Ceris stopped in front of what looked like an abandoned pub. With a brief glance at us, she pushed the heavy doors open and walked in. Victor went in with her while we waited outside.

Micah nudged me with his elbow. "Come on." He pointed his chin to the corner of the building and disappeared into another alley.

Curious, I took two steps forward and looked at the alley. It was narrow and had a single door at the end. Micah turned the knob on it and entered the building. Cursing my damned curiosity, I followed him.

We walked down a short corridor lined with doors—a

closet, an employee area, a kitchen, and restrooms, and found the door leading to the heart of the pub. Slowly, Micah reached for my hand and together we crossed the door.

The pub transformed into a ballroom. It was wide with a tall ceiling, and I was sure it didn't fit inside the building we had just entered.

"What the ...?" I muttered.

But that wasn't all. The ballroom was full of beautiful people in elegant gowns and tuxedos, everyone laughing and dancing and drinking champagne. A band—with singers, dancers, and guitar and piano players—played from a stage along the back wall.

In the middle of the ballroom, a woman danced with her arms up high and her hips moving all around. She threw her head back and let out a loud laugh, one that seemed to be contagious, as everyone else in the ballroom laughed even more. She lowered one of her arms and a flute of champagne appeared in her hand.

Ronen.

The goddess of entertainment was as beautiful as the other goddesses with her strawberry blond haircut in an asymmetric bob—at her chin on one side and at her shoulders on the other. Her body was as perfect as the other goddesses too. However, Ronen seemed to have more curves —bigger breasts and wider hips.

The group around her seemed enthralled by her. In fact, everyone in here did, as if this was her party and everyone had to please her.

She saw Victor and Ceris among the guests and smiled at them.

"Brother! Sister! It's so good to see you!" Her voice slurred like she was completely drunk.

"I don't know why but I didn't think gods could get drunk," I whispered.

"Only if we drink an entire liquor store," Micah returned.

"Oh."

Ceris leaned down closer to Ronen and said something we couldn't hear over the loud music, small chattering, and clank of glasses. But from the wrinkle on Ceris's usually immaculate forehead, I guessed her words weren't too nice.

Ronen let out a loud laugh and swatted Ceris's hand away.

Beside me, Micah stiffened. With his hand still on mine, he pulled me closer.

"What is it?"

"Demons," he hissed, looking to the pub's windows and doors.

Then Ronen's smile faded and it all went away. The fancy ballroom, the elegant guests, the champagne, the band. It all just disappeared, leaving in its wake a pub that looked as broken and neglected as the outside. Broken tables, broken chairs, broken bar, dim lights, and a lot of missing bulbs. And only Ronen and us on the inside.

It was all an illusion. Magic.

"Demons are here," Ronen whispered, her eyes wide.

Ceris and Victor exchanged a look with Micah. He nodded. And the next thing I knew, the world revolved. I blinked and found myself standing in what looked like the National Park in D.C., although this park was black, dead, with fallen buildings and monuments and debris. Lots and lots of debris.

"What the hell?" I snapped, turning to Micah, but then I saw everyone else standing behind him. Ceris, Victor, Maho,

Sol, Keisha, Alice, and even a drunken Ronen. She looked around and started laughing again.

"We decided it was best to teleport out of there once we sensed the demons closing in on us," Victor said, letting go of Ronen's arm.

She swayed and laughed some more. "Where did the party go?" She looked around. "Man, this place doesn't look like fun."

Well, so far Ronen was living up to the whole patron-of-entertainment thing.

"Ronen, focus!" Ceris exclaimed, her tone sharp, her eyes even sharper.

"Why, sister?" Ronen shouted, followed by another loud laugh. "The world is going up in flames and I want to have fun while I can."

"That's the thing," Victor said. "We want to prevent the world from going up in flames."

The amusement on Ronen's face faded. "Prevent it? I'm afraid that's impossible."

"Ronen, listen to us," Micah spoke up. "United, we can fight Imha and Omi. We can win."

She actually stopped and looked at him. At everyone. "That's quite a team you've got. I'm afraid it's not enough."

Ceris nodded. "We have more allies on our side and we'll get even more. It will be enough."

"Just ... come with us and hear us out," Victor said, extending his hand to her.

Ronen stared at his hand, studying it as if it could bite her if she gave in to it. "I'm not sure."

Ceris put her hands on her waist. "Do you have anything else to do? Just listen to what we have to say. If you think it's not worth it, we'll let you go and you can conjure fake parties until Imha comes and kills you herself."

Ronen winced. But it seemed Ceris's hurtful logic got through the goddess's barriers.

She rested her hand on Victor's. "Okay."

They all disappeared, and then Micah turned to me, his hand awaiting mine. "Let's go, darling."

With a sigh, I grabbed his hand and let him teleport us out of there.

14

———

NADINE

THE DAYS WERE PASSING, AND NOT MUCH WAS HAPPENING.

After we had come back from Russia with Ronen, it took her a while to realize staying with us and fighting was the best option. She seemed ready to bolt at any moment. And God knows what would happen then. Imha might capture her and squeeze the location of our hideout from her. However, Micah thought it was just nerves mixed with withdraw from her parties and booze.

After a long meeting with Victor, Ceris, Maho, Sol, Ronen, Izaera, Zelen, Keisha, and Alice—anyone seen Micah? Nope—I retreated to my room just as the pain became unbearable. I couldn't keep from shaking. I didn't want them to see me in pain again.

I fought through the pain as it increased and increased. An hour—or two?—later, I was biting my pillow to hide my screams. My body shook and my mind felt like mush.

This was the second time in three days.

I was dying. That must be it. I couldn't think of any other explanation.

After another hour, the pain lessened enough for me to take a long breath without crying out.

A knock came from my closed door. "Nadine?" It was Alice.

"Yes?" I said, my voice raw.

"Lady Ceris said the scouts are coming, and she thought you would like to talk to them."

Groaning, I sat up. "I'll be right there."

I stood from my bed, made sure I didn't look like I was in any pain, and headed for the living room. I gritted my teeth with every step, but it was better than feeling like my body was exploding in a million pieces.

Careful with my movements, I sat in an armchair. Around me, I saw Alice, Keisha, Ceris, and Victor. "Where are the others?" And by that I meant, where was Micah? Izaera and Zelen never stayed long, and I didn't care that much about Maho, Sol, and Ronen—as long as they were behaving and helping us.

"They left right after the meeting," Victor said.

"Still looking for allies?" I asked.

"What else?" replied Ceris, her voice cold. Ugh. Someone was in a bad mood.

To answer her question, I could think of other things to do, like plan a war with the resources we had instead of looking for allies for months. I agreed we needed numbers, but we didn't have forever to put together an army.

"They are here," Ceris said, opening the door.

Two of our scouts walked into the apartment.

"Any news?" Victor asked after the scouts took their usual stoic position in the middle of the living room.

"It seems Imha and Omi have been holed up in a current

villa in England," the blond scout said. "But the demons are still destroying everything in their path."

"Is there a pattern to their destruction?" Ceris asked.

The blond scout shook his head. "No, my lady."

"I did have some progress with the Death Lords, though," the tall scout said.

Ceris brows shot up. "What did you say, Rihan?"

"I trailed the Death Lords for two days, and then they disappeared near one of the underworld's main entrances."

"Wait." Victor raised a finger, as if asking for a minute. "You were following the Death Lords?"

"Y-yes," Rihan replied, and for the first time, I saw his usual soldier-like expression falter. "Just as Lord Mitrus asked me."

Ceris and Victor exchanged a long, meaningful look. Uh-oh.

"Rihan, I need you to stop trailing the Death Lords," Victor said. "You and the others are to focus on Imha and Omi only."

Rihan bowed his head. "Yes, my lord."

"Thank you for the update," Victor said, his voice strained. "If anything changes, please let us know."

"You can go now," Ceris said, waving her hand to the front door.

After bowing, the scouts hurried out the door. Ceris paced the living room, as if counting her steps. After an entire minute, she exploded.

"I can't believe it!" she yelled and the walls shook. "I'm gonna kill him."

Victor sighed. "Let's not be too hasty. Mitrus might have a good reason for changing our orders."

"He better," Ceris hissed.

Afraid to disrupt Ceris's latest breakdown, Alice, Keisha, and I went to the gym and left Victor alone to deal with his soulmate.

Alice closed the door. "What was all that about?"

I shrugged. I didn't know, but something told me the reason Micah changed the scouts' orders wasn't good enough. If I was right, he was in big trouble with Ceris and Victor.

15

MICAH

I STEPPED INTO THE APARTMENT AND MY PERSONAL RECEPTION was waiting for me. I was getting used to it. This time, though, Ceris's and Levi's expressions were harder, madder.

"What happened?" I asked.

"You tell us," Ceris said. Her face was mad, her body language was tense, but her voice was calm. Too calm. A bad sign.

"Tell you what?"

"Where were you, Mitrus?" Levi asked.

I clenched my jaw. What now? They would control my every move? I wouldn't tell them where I had been. Being in the underworld with Morgan was my one solace, my one place of peace, where I could relax and be myself and not worrying about disappointing anyone. They wouldn't take that away from me.

"It's none of your business," I snapped.

"I think it is," Ceris said, her tone cracking a little. "We just talked to our scouts, and they told us you changed our last directive before they left. Why?"

By the Everlast.

I ran a hand through my hair and glanced around. The gym door was closed, and I could hear grunts and clanks of wooden swords. Nadine was busy with the others. "I … I can't shake the feeling that I can get my hands on the Cup of Life, but I need to find out where the Death Lords are hiding first."

She dropped her arms and shook her head. "That again? I thought you were done with that."

I gritted my teeth. "I would like to think I am, but the truth is I'll never be. Until the day we finish the Soul Oath and Nadine d—" I pressed my lips together, hating to utter this word out loud. "And Nadine dies, I won't be done with it. I spend all my time thinking about how I can save her, how I can make sure she won't die."

Ceris narrowed her eyes at me. "You're admitting you're not helping us with this war?"

Levi rested a hand on her arm. "Ceris, calm down. Think about all you went through to get us—me—back. All you did. He's in love with her; he can't help it."

Ceris huffed and crossed her arms. "That isn't the same. You're my soulmate, Levi. Nadine is a mortal, and even if she doesn't die with the Soul Oath, she'll die someday. Have you ever thought of that, Mitrus?"

"That's why I need to find the Death Lords and the Cup of Life." I sighed, exhausted with arguing all the time. "I swear I thought I was done with it. I hadn't thought about going after the Death Lords since I came back." That was a half-lie since Rok had been out all the time, trying to find the Death Lords for me. But my raven was never able to track them for long. "Then I saw the scouts here, and they have been good at tracking Imha and Omi and their demons. I thought … I thought they could find the Death Lords. I didn't dare to hope, though. If Rihan came back telling me he had found them, then I would act. Then I would have talked to you both before acting."

Ceris and Levi exchanged a long glance, and I wished I could read their minds.

"Rihan didn't find them," Ceris said, looking at me with her icy blue eyes. "He said their trail was short and cold. He searched for two days and found nothing."

It was a like a dam had burst in my chest. I felt the hope rushing out like unconstrained water, leaving me dry.

"I'm sorry," Levi said.

I gulped, swallowing the hurt and the pain. "Thank you," I whispered.

16

———

NADINE

FINALLY, A WEEK AFTER WE FOUND RONEN, I FOUND LUA. HER symbol had stayed in the same spot for over an hour. Ceris wanted to wait and see if she stayed there, while Sol, eager to find his soulmate, wanted to go right away in case she decided to move again.

In the end, we waited another hour, then geared up and went to get Lua.

Ceris, Victor, Micah, Maho, Ronen, Sol, Alice, Keisha, and I popped into a dark desert. There were sand and sand dunes everywhere we looked.

"What an odd place to be," I said under my breath.

Micah glanced at me. "Before the darkness took over, this place was ideal to look up at the sky and admire the moon and the stars."

I stared at him. I hadn't expected anyone to answer, much less him. Why did he keep surprising me? And the things he said? It was as if he had tailored his words to gut me.

"Anyone sensing her?" Victor's voice was loud and clear.

I averted my eyes from Micah's and watched the other gods.

"No," Maho said. He turned to me. "Are you sure she's here?"

Hating when they doubted me, I frowned. "I am."

Ceris produced the map and handed it to me. "Check again."

I took the map from her and unrolled it. I gasped as Lua's symbol faded before my eyes. "It's disappearing."

"What do you mean?" Sol came to stand behind me and looked at the map over my shoulder, but like the others, he couldn't see anything.

"It's ..." I counted four seconds before it disappeared completely. "It's gone."

As if I had hit him with my bare hands, Sol took a wide step to the side. "She's not here anymore?"

"No ..." I looked at the map again. Her symbol was nowhere to be seen. "I'm sorry."

Ceris exhaled loudly. "It's okay. It's not your fault. We knew Lua hasn't stopped for long in the same place, but we had to risk it."

"All right," Victor said. "There's nothing here. Let's go back."

"Wait," Keisha said. She stood atop of a sand dune about a hundred yards from us. "I see something."

We all walked closer to her. From the top of the dune, we could see the end of the desert in the distance and the flickering lights of a small town. To the east, what looked like a dark shadow grew closer and closer to the town.

"What's that?" I asked.

"Demons," Micah said from beside me, his voice filled with rage.

"They are going to attack that town," Alice said. "Just like they did to my town."

I shifted my gaze to Ceris. "Unless we stop them."

She cut me a look that said all I needed to know. Since it wasn't our priority, she didn't want to go, but she wouldn't say that out loud.

Victor nodded, his gaze on the long, dark shadow moving across the desert. "Let's do it."

The gods teleported us closer to the demons. We crouched behind the top of a dune and watched as the hundreds of demons marched toward the town.

"It's now or never," Maho said.

Hundreds against nine. It was a good thing some of us were powerful.

We stayed low and hidden by the darkness, approaching the demons from behind. When we were within reach, we attacked. By the time they recovered from our surprise attack, we had already advanced through their formation, but they still came at us from all sides. Our group spread out and met the demons with fierce determination.

I didn't know how much time passed or how many demons I had already taken down—a dozen? Maybe even two dozen?—when I noticed I was a little farther away and surrounded. Slowly, I turned and counted eleven demons in the first line. There were more behind them, and even more coming to watch—or make sure they didn't miss me.

I gulped. Even though I was a good fighter, I couldn't take on half an army of demons by myself. I knew that.

No time to panic. With a growl, I raised my sword and readied myself. I spread my legs open and gripped the hilt of my sword tighter. Two demons broke from the circle and ran at me. Moving faster than I had ever moved, I slashed the throat of the first and pierced the chest of the second. I pulled my sword free and parried the claw of a third demon. Then a fourth was behind me and a fifth was advancing. Again, I didn't overthink, I just moved. Slash, parry, dodge, duck, pierce. I got rid of two of them, but then two more came at me. One swiped its claws and I stepped back right into the claws of another one. It slashed, cutting diagonally across my shoulder blade. I clamped my mouth, swallowing a scream, and swung my sword, cutting off the demon's arm. It roared and lunged at me like a lion, its pointy teeth bared and its remaining claws ready in a hook. I parried its attack, but then three other demons were on me. One closed its claws around my hurt shoulder, while the other grabbed my ponytail and pulled my head back. Another one slapped my arm down hard, making me lose the grip on my sword.

Panic rose in me.

The demons forced me to my knees and the armless demon let out a sound like a sick chuckle as it lifted its remaining claws to strike.

No, no, no, no.

I couldn't die yet. I wasn't ready. I had to help Micah and Victor and Ceris win the war. I needed to make sure the Soul Oath was finished the right way.

I jerked against the demons' hold and tried reaching into my boots, where I had stashed daggers.

With a loud roar, the demon let his arm fall. I closed my eyes.

But the claw never came. Instead, the demon grunted and was knocked to the side. I snapped my eyes open. A black bolt flew over my head, hitting the demon holding my shoulders. The bolt exploded in its face and it stumbled back before falling over other demons. Three more quick black bolts followed, getting rid of most of the demons around me.

Micah.

I wanted to look at him, to tell him thanks, but instead, I crawled to my sword. A demon stepped on it as my hand closed around the hilt. With a wicked, sharp-toothed grin, the demon kicked high, hitting my chin and sending me flying backward. My vision blackened and my head spun. I hit the sandy ground, right in the middle of more demons.

The demons stood over me, ready to finish me again. Their sharp claws and pointed teeth bared, closing in on me.

"Hang on," Keisha yelled somewhere to my side.

I lifted my head enough to see her dashing through a throng of demons, coming at me. From the other side, the black bolts resumed, knocking the demons down.

In the chaos of the battle, Micah and Keisha didn't see each other.

"Stop," I tried yelling, but my throat hurt, and my voice was barely above a whisper. "Keisha, stop!"

It was like watching in slow motion. Keisha stood beside me, a huge demon in front of her. One of Micah's bolts sailed through the air and hit the same demon square in the back. The demon fell to the side, and the next bolt hit Keisha.

Her eyes widened as she looked down at the hole in her chest.

"Oh, gods," I heard Micah's voice from afar.

Keisha's limp body fell beside me.

"Keisha!" I screamed, trying to get to her, but there were still demons everywhere.

Not thinking, only feeling immense rage and despair, I threw my hands out and the white light flashed from them, spreading around me in a wide circle, taking out every demon nearby.

I had to roll out from under a gross, heavy body to reach her. But by then, she was already gone.

A lump rose in my throat. I touched her shoulder. "Keisha?"

She had fallen over a dead demon. Her head lolled back and her eyes were open, staring at nothing. Her arms and legs were unnaturally bent.

"Oh my God," I whispered. A sob rippled through me.

"By the Everlast," Victor said.

I blinked and, through the unshed tears, saw that they were all standing to my right, staring at Keisha and me. Victor, Ceris, Maho, Sol, Ronen, Alice, and Micah.

Micah. Who had killed her.

His jaw ticked and the muscles in his neck tense. He shifted his gaze to me, his dark eyes shining with grief. "I'm ... I'm so sorry."

17

─────

I still couldn't believe what I had done.

Gods, I had killed Keisha.

"What are we going to do with her?" I asked in a voice too small, too weak to be mine.

"We should take her with us and give her a proper burial," Levi suggested. "Like I wish we could have done for Morgan."

I nodded, not trusting myself to speak again.

Levi picked her mangled body up and teleported back to NYC. There, he used magic to dig a grave in a small patch of dead grass. A knot formed in my chest as he lowered her body into the hole and filled it with dirt again.

"We should come back later with the others to finish the rites," Maho said.

They started walking back to the apartment, but I stood there, staring at the improvised grave.

Levi turned back. His hand rested on my shoulder. "I'm sorry."

I shook my head. "Not more than I am," I grunted. "I can't believe ... I can't believe I did this."

"It was an accident."

"That doesn't change the fact that I killed her."

Levi scoffed. "You sound like Nadine talking about Morgan."

I turned around and glared at him. "That was different. Morgan wasn't himself. He had to be stopped. Nadine did the right thing." I glanced at the grave again. "Keisha was ... she didn't deserve to die."

Levi squeezed my shoulder. "I don't know what to say other than it's okay to feel frustrated and mad, and it's okay to mourn her."

Frustrated and mad didn't even begin to cover what I was feeling. One more screwup. A huge one at that.

Levi and Maho left, but I stayed outside for a long time.

I wasn't ready to go inside. I wasn't ready to face Nadine.

But I couldn't run from her forever.

Slowly, I made my way to the apartment.

As expected, everyone was in the living room, and Nadine was seated on the couch, her body looking as limp as Keisha's.

As soon as she saw me, she straightened and her stare could drill a hole in my forehead.

"You killed her," Nadine whispered. The hatred in her eyes, the disappointment. That hurt more than the Black Thorn piercing my heart. More than the poisonous web spreading across my chest.

"You know I didn't mean to," I said. "I would never do that."

Ceris stepped forward and faced me, her eyes hard, cruel. "I'm not so sure."

I flinched as if she had hit me. "Excuse me?"

"First, you almost get Victor hurt. Then, you change our scouts' orders. And now you get one of ours killed? I'm sorry, Mitrus, but since you came back from Nasya's island, you've been elusive. I'm not sure we can trust you anymore."

I looked from her to Levi to Nadine. They had the same wariness in their eyes, the same distrust as Ceris. So did Maho, Sol, Ronen, and Alice.

"You can't be serious."

"Do I look like I'm not serious?" Ceris asked. No, she didn't.

Ironic how the goddess that screwed us over a few months ago now was the one accusing me of screwing them over.

The worst part was I didn't know anymore. I didn't want to hurt them, but when an opportunity came, I couldn't think of not doing what the Death Lords asked me to. As much as it angered me to do their bidding, to bow down to them, I couldn't see another solution. I had to let Nadine go, but I couldn't. Even if she hated me, even if she never wanted to see me again, I couldn't let her die.

However, this time it had nothing to do with the Death Lords and their elusive deal. This time, I had made a big mistake.

Levi walked to his soulmate's side and caught her hand in his. "Ceris, you're exaggerating."

"Am I?" she snapped.

"Yes, you are," Levi said. "What happened today ... it was an accident. A terrible accident. It wasn't Mitrus's fault. You know that."

"What about the rest?"

"Misunderstandings." Levi looked at me, his bluish-green eyes serious. "I trust Mitrus. He wouldn't do anything to jeopardize everything we have worked for." He sighed. "Unfortunately, accidents happen and today we witnessed a big one."

Ceris pulled her hand free of Levi's grasp and took a step back as if it hurt to touch him.

I looked at Nadine. "I'm so sorry."

A tear rolled down Nadine's cheek. Without another word, she stood and marched to her bedroom. Ceris followed her, but instead, she went to her room at the end of the hall.

"Give them time," Levi said. "They will understand."

Would they? Would they not only understand but also forgive me?

I shook my head. Not even I could forgive myself, so why should they?

I turned around and headed to the door.

"Where are you going?" Maho asked.

"I ... I need fresh air," I said before leaving the apartment.

———

I HAD ALREADY DRUNK AN ENTIRE WHISKEY BOTTLE WHEN I summoned Morgan to my lair.

"I killed Keisha," I said as soon as he shimmered into existence in front of me. Morgan stared at me with wide eyes and an open mouth. I got another bottle from the bar, opened it, and downed half of it in one gulp. "It was an accident, but I killed her nonetheless."

Morgan finally closed his mouth and sat on one of the chaise lounges. "What happened, my lord?"

I told him all about our day. Finding Lua's symbol, going to the desert, not finding Lua there, but seeing demons preparing to attack. Nadine getting swarmed by demons and losing, my desperation to get to her and help her, and not seeing Keisha.

Screaming, I threw the bottle at the wall. Shards of glass and liquid flew everywhere.

Morgan gasped.

Slowly, I backed away from the mess and plopped down on the other chaise lounge. With a wave of my hand, the broken glass and spilled liquid were gone. It was as if it had never happened.

"I can sense her here in the underworld," I said. "She's confused and upset." Of course she was upset. Her ally had killed her. I would be raging, wreaking havoc, breaking everything, and punching everyone.

I felt so weak.

God of the dead and death and underworld, my ass. Right now, I was fucked-up Micah who didn't know what to do next.

Breaking the silence, Morgan asked in a careful tone, "What about Nadine, my lord?"

"She hates my guts right now, as she should. Maybe now she'll stay away from me for good."

Morgan tsked. "I doubted she hates you, my lord. She knows it was an accident."

I was so fucking tired of talking about this subject, of hearing from Levi and Morgan that it had been an accident. It didn't change the fact that I had killed a hero. This shit wasn't a game. Killing friends wasn't something I could just push aside.

"She used magic again today."

Morgan gaped at me. "Really?"

"Yeah. After I ... I killed Keisha. I think Nadine entered some kind of rage mode or something, and she just blasted out. All the demons in a twenty-yard radius collapsed. Despite the circumstances, it was incredible."

"You know, my lord, I've been thinking a lot about what is happening to Nadine." He stood and started pacing. "I remembered reading about a legend of a group of ladies who were similar to heroes. It was many years ago and I don't remember the exact details."

I sat up. "You read it in one of your books?"

"No. I read it when I visited a high priest in France. He had an incredible collection of books about the creed, and he told me he knew of a hidden place where several high priests from all around the world stashed sacred books for safekeeping, books that explained the history and forgotten legends of The Everlasting Circle."

A sliver of hope ran through my veins. "Do you know where this hidden place is?"

"He didn't want to tell me, my lord, but I can try to find out."

"How?"

Morgan smiled. "Well, my lord, he should be somewhere around the underworld. I can ask him."

Despite myself, I smiled too. Finally, something to look forward to.

———

"You weren't gone for long," Ceris said when I entered the apartment. She was seated on the couch, drinking a glass of wine and reading a book.

If I hadn't seen the book was about the creed, I could have sworn Ceris was a rich housewife, reading a romance novel, as if all was normal with the world.

Levi was pacing behind the sofa, also with a book in hand, but now his eyes were on me, and I could see Maho, Sol, and Ronen in the kitchen. Though I tried not using this kind of power with her, I sensed for Nadine. I found her in her bedroom with Alice.

"I think I know what is happening to Nadine and where we can find more books, better books, that might explain it."

Levi closed his book. "What? Where?"

"What do you think is happening to her?" Ceris asked.

"Morgan vaguely remembers of a legend about a group of ladies who were similar to heroes. We interrogated a high priest and—"

Levi raised his hand. "Wait, wait. You and Morgan interrogated a high priest? Just now? How?"

I almost rolled my eyes. "The guy is dead, okay? It was easy finding his soul in the underworld. I summoned him, and Morgan and I talked to him." I left out the part where the high priest didn't want to tell us anything, but when I promised to send him to the fiery pits of the underworld if he didn't help, he finally told us everything he knew. "This high priest told us there is a secret underground room in the library at the Saint Catherine's Monastery in Sinai in Egypt, where high priests hid sacred books."

"I don't see how these two facts are connected," Ceris said, always the fucking pessimist.

I stifled a groan. "Morgan *thinks* they are connected. Isn't that enough?"

"Not really."

This time I groaned. "Whatever. I'm going there."

"Wait," Levi said. "Do you even know the state of this library? Is it still standing?"

"No, but nothing a quick teleportation won't solve. And

even if it's not standing, I can try to find something in the wreckage."

Levi sighed. "I'm guessing you want to go right now?"

I crossed my arms. "The sooner, the better."

"Can I at least convince you to go tomorrow, after we're rested from the battle and during daylight?"

My brows shot up. "We?"

"Yes, we," he said. "I'm coming with you."

With her mouth agape, Ceris stood. "What?"

Levi looked at her, his expression passive. "I'm going on an important mission with my brother. Hope that we'll find what we're looking for."

Ceris pressed her lips together and her cheeks grew red. With a huff, she marched out of the living room.

I had to bite my cheek not to laugh. Then I glanced at Levi; he was serious and calm. I sighed. "Thank you."

He shrugged and returned to his book.

18

NADINE

EVEN THOUGH MY BODY AND MIND WERE EXHAUSTED, IT WAS hard to fall asleep. And after my latest nightmare—which involved Keisha and Micah—I couldn't go back to sleep.

In my dream, Micah had turned against us and killed us all one by one, starting with Keisha. He saved me for last and took his time between saying sweet things in my ear, which in another situation would have made me kiss him, and torturing me.

So, at four thirty in the morning, I was in my workout clothes, in the gym, hoping to burn off some energy so I could go back to sleep—nightmare-less—later.

I turned on the treadmill and ran. I focused on keeping my mind clear, my only attention on the rhythm of my breathing and the soft thud of my footsteps.

Almost an hour of *nothing* passed.

"Morning, darling." Micah's voice startled me, and I tripped, almost falling from the treadmill.

Cursing, I hopped off and turned to him, intent on ignoring him because if I let myself stay near him, I would lash out. I would breakdown and accuse him of things I knew weren't his fault.

Then I saw him and my heart skipped. I froze in place, my next breath stuck in my throat.

It wasn't even his unnatural good looks that had stopped me—he looked fresh and clean, as if he had just taken a shower and shaved. The black pants and black tee and bare feet made him looked relaxed. And his face ... I couldn't even think when paying attention to the sharp lines of his perfect face. What had stopped me and disarmed me was the tray in his hands.

"What's that?" I asked, glancing at the tray.

He stared at it. "I thought it was obvious. Waffles, eggs, toast, and coffee. Breakfast?"

I swallowed. "You made all that?"

He nodded. "Just now. Brought to you fresh from the oven."

After what he had done, I wanted to hate him. I wanted to scream at him. But after my shock had passed, after I accepted I was mourning and that I *had* to mourn Keisha, I admitted it hadn't been Micah's fault. I knew deep in my heart he had never meant to hurt her, and it was terrible of me to blame him for it.

Like him, I had killed one of ours and I knew how that guilt, that weight, could eat at one's soul and mind.

I pressed my lips together and shook my head once. "Why?"

He tilted his head to the side. "I ..." He set the tray on one of the weight-lifting benches. "Look, I know you hate my guts right now, and I want you to know that I understand why you hate me. The Fates know there are too many reasons for that." He ran a hand through his hair and sighed. "I came in here with a peace offering, knowing all too well that it was a long shot. A really long shot. So, here it is. Your breakfast." He picked up one of the coffee mugs from the tray, and then turned toward the door.

Now I felt like the biggest jerk.

"Wait," I said. He stopped and glanced at me over his shoulder. "Hmm, thanks."

"You're welcome." I thought he was going to keep going. Instead, he whirled on his heels and faced me again. "I ... I also came in here to tell you something."

I raised one eyebrow. "Oh?"

Micah cupped his mug with both hands. "I'm leaving in a few minutes."

The air was knocked out of my lungs. He was leaving? Again?

I tried to compose myself and relax my shocked expression. "May I ask where you're going?"

He averted his eyes. "All you have to know is that I'm going on a mission with Levi, and, hopefully, we'll be back in a day or two."

All you have to know ...

That stung. It was like after everything I had done for them, after all we had been through together, I was still a disposable piece on the game board. They didn't need me. They didn't want me here. They couldn't care less about what happened to me. Why share anything important with Nadine? Because she didn't matter.

"All right," I said, noticing how my voice wavered and feeling completely embarrassed for it. His gaze came back to mine and I held his stare. Firm and unflinching.

"I just ... I wanted to say goodbye this time, before leaving."

I held my breath. Here he was breaking my heart while being so thoughtful. Why couldn't I really hate him? It would be so much easier. "Good luck," I whispered.

A muscle in his jaw ticked and he nodded. "Thanks."

"That's too much food." I pointed to the tray. "If you're not leaving right now, and if you don't mind the current company, it would be okay for you to eat some." That had been the lamest attempt at peace in the history of our world. God, I was so lame.

One corner of Micah's lips tugged up. "To be honest, I wasn't going to eat anything right now, but I think I'll make an exception because of the current company."

And just like that, we sat on the floor, one on each side of the bench, and ate breakfast in a comforting silence, simply enjoying being together without bickering or pushing each other's buttons.

19

MICAH

LIKE THE REST OF THE WORLD, THE LIBRARY AT THE SAINT Catherine's Monastery was in ruins. Although, for once, it didn't seem to be because of Imha and her minions. It simply looked as if it had been abandoned for too many years and left to the negligence of time and weather.

"How old is this place?" Levi asked as we walked toward what looked like the main gate.

I scoffed. "Too old."

The narrow entrance passage was covered in rubble. The stone walls had crumbled and littered the access. Using our magic, Levi and I jumped past the stones to a more open area, which under so much destruction looked like a courtyard.

"I think it's through here." Levi turned to the right, leading to an even bigger open space—another courtyard. Again, the ground was littered with the crumbling walls and broken stones.

Before coming here, we had looked for maps and images of this place in old books and magazines. We sort of knew where the library used to be, though we weren't sure if the secret underground room was underneath the library or elsewhere.

We used magic again to skip past the debris and ended up facing a small chapel.

I stopped and looked inside the abandoned chapel. "Isn't it odd that books of our creed would be hidden in a Catholic church?"

Levi glanced inside the building. A big crucifix hung precariously from the farthest wall. "Perhaps that's why they were hidden here. Because this is the last place anyone would look for them."

"Perhaps," I muttered.

Beyond the chapel, there was another building—curiously intact. The library.

Carefully, I opened the door and stepped inside. Despite some shelves tilted to the side, supported by walls or other shelves, and a few scattered books and papers, the place looked undamaged.

"Now we look for a secret door leading down," I said.

Levi nodded and went to the right. I turned to the left and started walking around the tables, desks, and shelves. I wasn't sure what I was searching for, but I looked under the desks, shelves, and rugs, behind frames on the walls and doors. The only sound inside the library was the creaking of the old, rickety wooden floor as we stepped on it.

After one hour, I met Levi at the back of the library.

"Anything?" he asked.

I shook my head. "Nope."

"It certainly won't be obvious." His gaze scanned the area around us.

That got me thinking ... "I have an idea." I headed toward

the entrance of the library and found what looked like a reception desk. I walked behind it and, as I expected, I found several file cabinets. I started opening them and tried to make sense of how things were sorted.

Levi opened a drawer from another file cabinet. "What are we looking for?"

"Anything about religions," I said, going for the R. After an endless minute, I pulled a card out. "Here. *Religions of the World.* Shelf R7, row fifty-four." I jumped over the desk and rushed to shelf R7 with Levi right behind me. Following the numbers, it was easy to find row fifty-four. "Here," I said, taking out volume one of twelve. There were twelve volumes of *Religions of the World.*

Levi rubbed the back of his neck. "Now what?"

"Wait," I said as I opened volume one and looked through the appendix. Not in this one. I found it in volume six. "Here." I pointed to the title on the appendix page. "The Everlast Creed," I read out loud, smiling.

Levi's brows shot to his hairline. "How ... I didn't think our creed would be listed in a rather modern book."

I flipped to the copyright page. "It isn't that modern. First edition published in 1795."

"Compared to our ages, very modern."

I snorted and flipped the book back to where the history of our creed began. I skimmed through it. "This shit is all wrong."

"What do you want? For them to tell the truth about us? Yeah, right." Levi tilted his head and tried to read the book with me. "What are you looking for?"

"I'm not exactly sure," I said, still skimming through the many pages of garbage.

A drawing of the creed's symbol took over an entire page,

and below it the caption said, "To find it, you just have to be close to the earth."

"That doesn't make sense," Levi said.

Didn't it?

I knelt and felt the old wooden floor. Then I saw it, a wider space between three boards, going under the shelf.

I shot to my feet. "Help me here."

Together, we pushed the shelf, moving it back until it wasn't over the boards. A few books fell on the floor, but we pushed them aside.

Levi and I knelt on the floor again and started pulling on the three boards. They came out easier than I thought they would. Below where the boards had been, a narrow and steep stone staircase led down.

"Whoa," Levi said. "I wasn't expecting this. How did you know?"

"I didn't." I smiled. "Let's just say I tried to do what Nadine would have done. She's always saving our asses and finding everything for us."

He smiled back. "That she does." He looked down at the stairs. "So each time a high priest wanted to come here, they had to do all this? That is a lot of work."

I shrugged. "Perhaps they didn't want it to be easy."

"Perhaps," Levi said. "Ready?"

I nodded. "Let's go."

The stairs were narrow and dark, but as we went down, the steps widened. Two sets of flights later, we arrived at a landing and the light coming from upstairs no longer illuminated the stairwell. On the wall to my left and right were unlit torches in sconces. I conjured a bolt of energy in my hand and lit those torches. Levi grabbed one of the torches and we walked the perimeter of the room lighting the rest of them.

We met in the center of the room.

"Damn," I whispered, glancing around. We were in a large cavern with a high ceiling and many, many shelves and books. The shelves along the walls went from the floor to the ceiling, and the shelves in the middle of the room were almost as tall and looked like they would tilt if we tried to jam one more book in them.

I got close to one of the shelves and used the torch to illuminate the books.

The History of the Everlasting Circle. There were seven different volumes.

The Real History of the Everlasting Circle. This collection had ten volumes.

Deities of the Everlasting Circle from A to K and *Deities of the Everlasting Circle from L to Z.*

All About Demons.

I kept walking.

There were several books about each of us; there were too many books about me. I wanted to pick up a few and skim through them, but that would only delay our main search.

In the back of the room, I found not books but scrolls.

"By the Everlast."

This shit was *old*. Most of the scrolls looked like they would crumble into dust if picked up, but what if what we were looking for were on them? Nobody had heard of any group of ladies in so long, it had to be old. Ancient even.

"There are some books on legends here," Levi's voice came from somewhere on my right. I found him a few shelves away, holding his torch high as he leaned over a shelf. "Here." He pointed to the books in front of him.

Legends of the Everlasting Circle.

Myth or Truth: the Stories behind the Legends.

The Real Legends of the Everlasting Circle.
Heroes: Born or Made?

I placed the torch on a makeshift sconce on the side of the shelf, pulled the book about heroes, and opened it to the appendix. "Here," I said, pointing to the heading of chapter eight: Why Ladies of Diana are confused with heroes.

"Ladies of Diana?" Levi asked. "It doesn't ring a bell."

I flipped the pages until I had chapter nine open.

Like heroes, the ladies of Diana possess an affinity with weapons, increased strength and stamina, and faster healing abilities. However, the ladies of Diana may possess other special abilities—depending on their ranking—that aren't available to heroes.

Sounding like the author was trying to sell heroes at a grocery store, the chapter went on mostly about heroes, listing their abilities.

I dropped that book. "We need to find a book about the ladies of Diana."

"All right," Levi said, turning. He started to the front of the room.

"Where are you going?"

"To see if they have some kind of cabinet file with all the volumes listed, like we found upstairs."

I nodded, but he didn't see it. That would be helpful, but if this place was supposed to be a secret, would they—whoever they were—keep a list of all the books and scrolls in here? I wasn't so sure.

Regardless, what we were looking for had to be around here. I knew it.

A few more minutes passed. By then, I was kneeling low on the floor, looking at the titles on the lower part of the shelf. As if it were calling, I turned around to the shelf at my back and stared right at it.

Diana: A Legend or a True Goddess?

What the fuck? A goddess?

I pulled the book to my lap and opened it. The first chapter was titled "Who is Diana?"

I quickly flipped to the right page.

Diana is said to have been a major goddess parallel to but outside the Everlasting Circle. Rumors are that she vanished many millennia ago for unknown reasons.

As the goddess of justice and wisdom and courage and honesty, Diana could pass judgment even over the gods and goddesses of the Everlasting Circle. A natural huntress, Diana was said to possess a powerful spear that could render anyone immobile while she assessed their sins—even gods.

A goddess outside the Everlasting Circle? That didn't make much sense.

I looked again at the appendix for the chapter on the ladies of Diana.

I sensed him two seconds before he spoke in my mind.

Miss me?

I growled. *What the hell are you doing here, Amiel?*

Aren't you happy to know we followed your aura again? And here I thought this was just the perfect opportunity to take out Mister Life and Balance.

I glanced at Levi. He was hunched in front of a desk buried under scrolls and piles of paper, searching for gods knew what.

I'm tired of your games. Show your face if your man enough.

Oh, that is exactly my plan.

What?

My mind didn't have time to process what the hell he was telling me, because he suddenly appeared a few feet from me.

"Hello, Lord Mitrus," Amiel said with a wicked grin. *My* wicked grin.

Body tensing, I jumped up and readied myself for a fight—feet apart and arms up in front of me.

Behind Amiel stood Jed, Keon, and Riel with equally crazed expression on their faces.

"Aren't you going to ask if we brought the cup?" Amiel asked.

The question had been on the tip of my tongue, but I resisted. I resisted because if I uttered those words, it meant I was considering killing Levi, and that wasn't right. That would never be right.

"What in the Everlast ...?" Levi's voice rang behind me. "What are you doing here?"

Amiel's grin widened. "I'm so glad you asked that, Lord Levi. I'm more than happy to answer that question."

I clenched my fists. "Amiel," I said, a warning tone.

"You see, Lord Levi, Lord Mitrus wasn't completely honest with you about what happened at Nasya's island," Amiel said. "He didn't tell you about our deal."

"Deal?" Levi muttered.

"A deal we're here to see through," Amiel said.

"What is he talking about, Mitrus?" Levi asked.

"Bullshit. That's what he's talking," I snapped.

Amiel chuckled. "The deal we made with Lord Mitrus was that he was free to have the Cup of Life to give to his precious Nadine. On one condition." The eyes shone evil. "He had to kill you."

"What?" Levi asked, his voice barely above a whisper. "Mitrus, what is he talking about?"

"You should check his pockets, Lord Levi," Amiel said. "I bet you'll find his weapon hidden there."

Levi stood by my side, his eyes two hard stones. "What the hell is he talking about?"

"I never agreed to his deal," I said, staring at Levi, hoping he saw the truth in my eyes. "I never agreed to it, I swear. When I thought about going after them, it was to try to steal the cup from them. Nothing else."

"Check his pockets," Amiel sang.

A frown appeared between Levi's brows and he reached into the pockets of my leather jacket. I groaned, but I let him search me. He found it in my jacket's inside pocket.

His hand trembled as he pulled it out and stared at it. "A Black Thorn?"

"They left it for me on the island, and ... I almost left it behind, but I thought I could use it against Imha. Later, I remembered that as much as I wish she were truly dead, I couldn't kill her. We need all of us alive."

"But you kept the damn thing in your pocket." His eyes widened. "This entire time? Since you came back from the island? You had a Black Thorn in your pocket the entire time?"

I didn't answer and he took my silence as a yes.

"Told you, Lord Levi," Amiel said. "He was plotting against you, and now he brought you here to us."

I roared and in less than a second conjured a large black bolt and let it fly. Amiel moved but not fast enough. The bolt hit him in the shoulder and he went flying backward, taking Jed with him. Keon and Riel were moving, and so was Levi.

He cast a shield in front of him and growled at me.

"I'm on your side!" I told him as I dodged small bolts from Keon and Riel.

Levi looked like he wasn't sure if he should believe me or not. And I didn't blame him.

I cast a shield of my own and channeled my power, conjuring another powerful bolt. I feigned to the left, making Keon and Riel believe I was coming for them. They got ready for me, but then I turned to the right and let the bolt fly. It hit Keon in the chest. The Death Lord started falling to the ground, but before he could hit the floor, his body erupted in black smoke.

One down for the count.

"Believe me now?" I asked Levi.

Still a little reluctant, Levi nodded then joined me in the fight. Just in time too, as Amiel and Jed regrouped and stared at us.

"We can end this pretty quickly," Levi said to me, his voice low. "If we join powers, they won't stand a chance."

"Let's do it, but ... I want Amiel alive."

Levi nodded once and then we cast one bolt with both our powers.

Amiel's eyes widened. "No!"

He took a torch from one of the sconces and threw it at a shelf. The fire caught instantly, and spread like a wave in the ocean.

"Fuck," I uttered.

Levi and I threw our super bolt. Amiel ducked behind Keon and Riel, who received the brunt of the spell. They became smoke and floated away.

The fire was spreading fast. I made to reach for the book about Diana, but Amiel spoke, making me stop.

"Look what I've got here." He held the Cup of Life. My heart stopped for a brief moment. "You want it? Then kill him." He pointed to Levi.

"I've got a better idea," I said, teeth bared. And I lunged for him.

Knowing this was the end, Amiel did something I couldn't undo. He threw the Cup of Life in the fire, making sure it tipped and the liquid spilled over. Then he opened his arms, as if waiting for me to end his life.

But I was frozen in place, watching as the Cup of Life was lost forever, consumed by the raging fire.

Levi acted. He threw a white bolt at Amiel's heart, killing the bastard.

And I stared at the Cup of Life, as if I could will it to float from the fire, gather the spilled and evaporated liquid, and come to rest in my hands by only the strength in my stare.

That was when we felt it. Demons surrounding the place.

"Let's go," Levi said, tugging my arm. "Mitrus, we need to go. Now."

A shelf behind us fell, and the fire billowed. Heat licked my skin and I flinched.

Briefly awakened from my stupor, I scanned the area. The book was nowhere to be seen. It was probably under the shelves, already consumed by fire.

My chest hurt. Suddenly, it was hard to breathe, and I didn't think it was because of the smoke and the fumes.

Levi grabbed the collar of my leather jacket. "Wake up, Mitrus. It's gone. The cup and the book are gone. And there are demons coming our way. Now, let's move."

Feeling as if I were leaving my soul to be burned by the fire, I nodded and followed him out of the library.

———

As soon as we were out in the open courtyard of the monastery, Levi and I teleported to a deserted island in the Bahamas. This place had once been beautiful with white sand, crystal blue water, and a bright, warm sun. Now it was dark, the sand was thick and gray, and the water was cold.

And Levi was watching me with even colder eyes.

"I'll give you one minute to explain before I kill you myself," he said, his tone flat.

I knew he wouldn't actually kill me. He needed me just as I needed him. We all needed each other. But the hurt in his eyes …

I shook my head and sighed. "All right, I'll tell you every-thing." And so I did. I told him what happened on the island, all the details, including the deal Amiel and the others wanted to do, the Black Thorn they left with me, and I even lifted my shirt to show the black web of poison spreading across my chest.

"What the …?" Levi took one step toward me, his gaze locked on the thing that could quite possibly kill me. "Does it hurt?"

I dropped my shirt and hid my wound. "Rarely."

"And how fast is it spreading?"

"About an inch every week or so."

He took in a sharp breath. "Do you think … what do you think will happen?"

"I have no idea." I shrugged. "We can't do anything about this right now, so let's focus on what matters most."

Levi nodded absently. "Demons showed up. There is only one way for them to have known where we were."

"We have a spy among us."

"To be honest, I thought it was you." I guess I should have felt appalled, but I wasn't. He had all the reason in the world to doubt me. Levi sighed, as if he was trying to exhale all the worry and frustration from his system. "Do you think whoever it is, is like Morgan was? Not in control of himself?"

"I honestly don't know." I summoned some courage and continued, "But I think I know how we can turn that around in our favor."

Levi raised an eyebrow and I told him my plan.

20

NADINE

After Micah had breakfast with me, he left with Victor, and I decided I was feeling a little better, so I took a shower and went back to bed.

Two hours later, Alice woke me up, saying it was too late to be sleeping and we needed to train. I cursed her out loud and was able to stay in bed for another hour—it wasn't every night, or day, that I slept without nightmares waking me up.

When I finally got up, it was almost lunchtime, so I took my time, ate lunch, waited a decent amount of time, and only then went to train with Alice.

"Finally," she muttered as I joined her in the gym.

However, an hour into training, my focus proved to be shot. I couldn't concentrate, and Alice kept getting painful hits on me.

"Ow," I cried as I hit the mat again.

"What's up with you?" Alice asked, her tone unfriendly.

"I'm just ... today isn't a good day, that's all."

She put her hands on her waist. "So, if you're having a bad

day when we're ready to march on Imha and Omi, we shouldn't go then?"

I rolled my eyes. "God, you sound like Ceris right now."

"Well, Lady Ceris is right."

I grunted. "Okay, I'm done for the day."

I shot up to my feet and heard Alice muttering about putting everything at risk by not fully committing as I exited the room.

Not fully committing? Hadn't the girl heard about all I had gone through for the creed? I shook my head, deciding to ignore the comment. She was frustrated because we were now one partner short, and I wasn't in warrior mode today.

I had no idea what mode, or mood, I was in today.

With a heavy sigh, I went to the kitchen to make some coffee and found Ceris there, taking a fresh pot off the coffeemaker.

"Want some?" she asked as she poured coffee into a mug.

I plopped down on a stool and crossed my arms on the island counter. "Yup."

She got another mug from the cabinet, served the coffee, and then handed it to me. "Here you go."

"Thanks," I mumbled.

She sat down across from me. "What's with that pout?"

"I don't have a pout."

She had a small smile on her lips. "Oh, that mood. I know who caused that. And the pout. What did Mitrus do this time?"

I opened my mouth to tell her ... what was I going to tell her? Not even I knew. In the end, I sighed and said, "He made me breakfast this morning." I closed my hands around my mug and inhaled the rich scent of coffee. "He then said he wanted to tell me goodbye properly this time and promised he would be back soon."

"All right. Shouldn't those actions make you, I don't know, feel relieved or content that he's reaching out?"

"They do. They did." I sipped from my mug, trying to sort through the mess of thoughts in my mind and feelings in my chest. "I just ... I don't know what to feel or what to do anymore. Not when it comes to him." I shook my head. "I'm not even sure why I'm telling you all this. It's not like you really care."

She lost the smile and a knot appeared on her wrinkle free forehead. "I know I can be a bitch sometimes, and I know we don't see eye-to-eye most of the time, but I'm still Cheryl. I'm still your friend."

I stared at her. "You have an odd way of showing it."

"I know." She sighed. "But it's the truth. When I was Cheryl, I got to know you, and you were my friend. A real friend. I kinda miss that." Her blue eyes shone and I could see in them that she was being honest. Or maybe she was a good liar.

"It's not that easy. To forgive and forget about everything that happened after that."

She let out a deep breath. "I know, but—" Suddenly, she tensed. "They are back."

We both shot up from our seats and rushed to the living room just as the front door opened with a bang.

Victor marched in several steps ahead of Micah. I gasped, taking in their singed clothes and the heavy smell of smoke.

"What happened?" Ceris asked, going to Victor.

Alice came from the gym, and Maho, Ronen, and Sol walked into the living room from the hallway that led to the bedrooms.

Fists clenched, Victor paced in front of her. And I watched Micah—his hand was red, as if he had burned it.

"Are you okay?" I asked, my voice low, careful.

He shook his head and averted his eyes.

Ceris glanced from Victor to Micah and back to Victor, the knot in her forehead deepening. "Someone say something!"

Victor halted. He turned to Micah with such tension in his body and so much rage and ice in his eyes. "Mitrus ..." He took in a long breath. "The Death Lords found us and said Mitrus was—is—working with them."

"What?" Ceris asked, her tone not as surprised.

I took a sharp breath, not believing what I was hearing. No. Micah would never work with the Death Lords. Not after all they had done to us.

Micah shook his head again. "It's a lie. You know that."

Victor advanced one large step, but then stopped himself again. "Do I? Do I really know that? I'm not sure anymore."

"Tell me what happened," Ceris asked, looking at her soulmate.

Victor's gaze fell on me before returning to Ceris. "It doesn't matter. Not now." He then puffed out his chest and lifted his chin. "Mitrus, you should leave. For good."

"What?" Micah and I asked in unison.

"I ... I don't know if I can trust you anymore, and until I can find out the truth, I don't want you near any of us."

"I can prove that I'm on your side," Micah said, his tone almost begging.

Victor shook his head. "No. It would be too damn easy for you to lie again, to try to twist the truth to make it look like an accident. If I'm to find out the truth, I want to do it alone."

Ceris glared at Micah. "You heard him. Leave."

"Wait, that's too much," I interjected. "How ... we have to talk about this. There must be an explanation." I turned to Micah. "Right?"

His dark eyes lost its usual amused shine and he averted his gaze. Oh, God.

"There's nothing to talk about." Victor's voice was hard. Dangerous. "The situation is well past the talking phase." Victor pointed to the door. "Leave, Mitrus. Now."

Micah sucked in a long breath and stared at Victor one more time before nodding and walking out. Without looking back. Without looking at me. Without saying goodbye.

The door closed behind Micah, and everyone stayed frozen in place for a minute. My brain was still playing catch-up, trying to understand what the hell had happened.

Victor let out a loud breath. "I need a shower." He turned toward the hallway, but I cut him off, blocking his path.

"First you tell me what happened."

"Not now, Nadine," he growled.

"Yes, now." I folded my arms over my chest. "The shower isn't going anywhere."

"I'm tired, I'm dirty, I'm hungry." He rubbed his eyes with the balls of his hands. "We can talk later."

I stomped my foot like a petulant child. "I don't care! Tell me now."

He sighed. "All you need to know is we can't trust Mitrus anymore. He was probably working with the Death Lords ever since he came back from Nasya's island."

I had heard them mention this place before. "What's Nasya's island?"

"It doesn't matter now."

"Stop treating me like I'm a child who will not understand

what's going on. Or are you not telling me because you also think I'm not an important part of this damn thing?"

He frowned. "Also? Who thinks ...?" He shook his head. "You're important to this war, Nadine, you know that."

"Then stop stalling and tell me."

"I won't tell you!" Victor raised his voice and I flinched. Ouch, that hurt. He sighed. "I swear to you if it made any difference, I would tell you, but it doesn't now. Unfortunately, what he did, and what we were doing earlier today doesn't matter anymore. All that matters now is I believe he betrayed us, even if only for a moment. We can't trust him now and we should move on."

"But—"

"Nadine," Ceris said. One word uttered with such power, an intense demand, a warning.

It didn't make sense. Victor and Micah had left like brothers, and they had come back as enemies. What the hell had happened? Why did I feel like they were hiding so much from me? From everyone?

I stepped aside and let them pass.

But this was not over. I would find out what happened, one way or another.

21

MICAH

Morgan didn't like my plan, but I didn't care. I was out of options. I needed to do something.

After two days of planning, I teleported to the edge of the hill in England, a hill that housed a large villa-like castle—the place I had heard Imha was calling her headquarters these days.

Demons upon demons dotted the landscape and guarded the tall stone fence around the villa. They saw me the moment I appeared and charged. I raised my hands, creating a barrier around me.

"I'm not here to fight," I said loud and clear. "I'm here to speak with Imha and Omi."

The demons stopped and looked at each other, unsure of what to think. Dumb things.

The sea of demons opened up, revealing Corinia, a lesser goddess under Maho. She walked toward me, a sly smile on her pale lips. "Well, well, what do we have here?"

I dropped my shield. "Working for Imha, huh? That's so unlike you."

"It's all about survival of the fittest, my lord. Imha and Omi have the upper hand, so here I am." She halted only three feet from me and flipped her long blond hair. Batting her lashes, she asked, "What are you doing here?"

"I want to talk to Imha and Omi."

"About?"

I growled. "Are you really asking me that?"

She bowed, though I knew it wasn't a real curtsy. "My apologies, my lord." She gestured to the path leading up the hill. "This way, my lord."

I followed her to the estate. The demons stepped back, watching me with hunger in their yellow eyes—hunger for fighting, for killing.

The villa was even more opulent from the inside. Fancy stone flooring, big chandeliers, velvet cushions and curtains, thick rugs, large paintings—just like Imha liked.

Corinia took me down a long hallway on the first floor. She knocked on the double doors, and they opened a second later.

Imha stood in the middle of what looked like a converted throne room. Omi was behind her, seated on one of the throne-like chairs.

"What a surprise," Imha said, smiling. She waved her hands to Corinia, dismissing her.

As soon as Corinia closed the double doors behind her, Omi stood. "Give me a good reason why I shouldn't use this in the next ten seconds?" He extended his hand and a Black Thorn appeared on his palm.

"I'm here to join you," I said, my eyes fixed on Imha. I hoped our past would speak for itself, and she would at least consider my proposition.

Her smile widened. "I thought you were on a honeymoon with your new best friend."

I scoffed. "You know Levi wasn't and never will be my friend. We just endured each other. This time was no different. We needed each other to find out who we were and locate our scepters. Now, I don't have to pretend to care anymore."

Omi snorted. "As if that was enough."

Imha clicked her tongue. "To be honest, I heard about your deal with the Death Lords. Planning on killing Levi, huh? So exciting! Though, apparently, it didn't work."

"Unfortunately, it didn't," I said through gritted teeth. "But I would like a chance to try again."

"I bet." Imha tilted her head. Her long, black hair fell to the side like a curtain. "This might be a good thing. Can you imagine? Chaos, war, and death ruling the world?"

Omi turned to her, his teeth clenched. "I don't like this."

She gave him a hard look and he retreated.

Throughout our history, Imha had had a hold over Omi, but it was nothing like this before. The way she quieted him with just a look was interesting and concerning.

Without her wicked smile, Imha returned her gaze to me. "I like the idea of having you by my side." The glint in her crazy eyes left no room for misinterpretation—the double meaning of having me by her side didn't escape me. I stifled a shudder. "But it won't be that easy. I want proof that you're on our side."

I expected as much. "What do you want me to do?"

She shrugged. "Surprise me. The bigger, the better."

I focused on my mission here and forced a sly grin of my own. "I have an idea."

22

NADINE

ALICE SWUNG HER ARM AND HER FIST SLAMMED INTO MY shoulder. I staggered back, a little disoriented.

"Sorry," she said, already sounding irritated. "If you weren't so distracted, I bet I wouldn't get one hit in."

True. Or at least it would have been harder for her. But as it was, I was distracted. Again. There was too much going on.

Everything had changed in the last three days. Keisha died, Micah left, we had a simple funeral for Keisha, and Victor continued to ignore my questions, so now I was ignoring him too.

Even Ceris, who I had actually made progress with in the friendship department, had become a bitch once again.

Last night, I had told her, "If you want to be my friend, then prove it to me. Tell me what happened between Micah and Victor. Tell me everything, including this damn Nasya's island that I heard you guys talking about."

She just shook her head and told me it was not for her to tell, and even if she could, she didn't think it was a good idea to worry me with things I couldn't change.

And there was our war progress too. It seemed stalled, at least from my end. I kept checking the map for Lua, but her symbol had disappeared in the desert and never reappeared again. Still, I looked, hoping she would emerge soon.

I shook my shoulders and came back to the present.

"I can't help it," I said to Alice.

"Then you'll be killed in the next battle."

I flinched. Keisha had been killed in the last battle. Then the next was me? And the next? Alice? Would our numbers dwindle until there was no one left to fight Imha and Omi?

Alice was right, though. If I didn't focus, I would be killed in the next battle. And I couldn't die. Not yet.

I closed my eyes and let out a long breath, trying to empty my mind. There was no family in the underworld, no guilt over Morgan's death, no disappointment over Micah leaving, no sadness over Keisha's death, no frustration with Victor and Ceris. There was only my adversary. One fight at a time.

Opening my eyes, I rolled my shoulders and readied myself—feet apart, knees bent, arms raised, fists closed.

Alice smiled, mirroring my stance.

I didn't leave room for thought. I lunged at her with all I had.

Then Ceris flew by the gym's door with Victor, Sol, Ronen, and Maho on her tail.

I halted, watching as they opened the front door with haste.

And Alice's fist hit my jaw.

Groaning, I stumbled back.

"Hey!" Alice cried. "I thought you were ready."

"I was," I said through the pain spreading across my face. "But something is happening." I pointed to the hallway and she turned to look, her brows furrowing. I walked past her and went to check it out. "What's up?"

"A scout is coming," Maho answered.

I frowned. "A scout? But he isn't supposed to come for another six days."

"Exactly," he said, his tone laced with concerned.

The blond scout hurried up the steps. He arrived at the apartment's door out of breath.

"What happened?" Ceris asked, ushering him in.

"It's Lord Mitrus," he said between long breaths. "I saw him this morning."

"And?" Victor asked.

"I saw him this morning while I was scouting one of Imha's bases."

I knew what he was saying, but my mind couldn't put one and one together. "What do you mean?" I asked, wanting to hear him say it out loud.

"He was with Imha," the scout said. I gasped. "I saw him entering the grounds, being escorted by Corinia, and then leaving, accompanied by Imha. She looked ... pleased with his presence."

My heart bled. I couldn't believe it. No, Micah wouldn't do that. He wouldn't turn his back on us. That didn't make sense.

"I can't believe it!" Ceris exclaimed so loud, her voice filled with so much rage the walls shook.

"Calm down." Maho put a hand on her arm.

"She's right to me mad," Victor said. "He betrayed us."

"You don't know that." The words rushed out of my mouth before I could stop them.

Ceris glared at me. "After all he did, what other evidence do you need?"

The scout cleared his throat. "Our spy says he was

working on a deal with Imha, though he doesn't know the details."

"By the Everlast," Ronen whispered.

I retreated a step.

"He wouldn't just join Imha and Omi," Maho said.

I took another step.

"Chaos, war, and death," Sol muttered. "We're doomed."

And another step.

"No, we aren't," Ceris said, her voice firm and confident. "We'll work through this. We'll make it."

Another step.

"What if Imha decides to squeeze him for information on us, on our plans?" Ronen asked, clenching and unclenching her fists.

"That ..." Ceris inhaled deeply. "That's a risk we can't control now."

One more step.

"What should I do, my lord?" the scout asked Victor.

Just one more step.

"Tell your spy to find out more about Mitrus and this deal," Victor answered. "We need all the information we can get."

The scout answered, but I didn't really hear him. I was already darting into my bedroom and closing the door. I leaned against the wall and took a deep breath.

It hurt, it all hurt. The pain started slow, but the burning was increasing. It was spreading. I gasped for air but nothing came.

Dizzy, I dragged myself to the bed and crawled in. I hugged Pinky, telling myself I could fight through the pain—the physical one, inexplicable one, and the one in my soul. The one that couldn't believe Micah had betrayed us.

A tear slid down my cheek, but I wiped it away as if it were poisonous. I wouldn't cry for him. He didn't deserve my tears.

The pain ricocheted and I bit my pillow, swallowing the scream.

It would be a long, painful night.

23

———————

MICAH

ANOTHER BOOM ECHOED IN MY EARS AND ANOTHER BALL OF FIRE descended on the small Italian town. I watched from the mountain as the orange and yellow consumed the houses and buildings. Women, children, and men ran, some crying, some yelling, some badly burnt. There was nowhere to go. They were trapped by the fire.

Aruhi appeared by my side. "It's done, my lord."

"Good," I said.

I waved my fingers at him and black snakes wrapped around him. He cried and jerked against the magical hold, but the snakes bit him and his body went limp, falling to the ground.

Forgetting the fallen lesser god, I watched the scene for hours until the fire was gone, leaving only charcoal behind.

I sighed, walked to Aruhi's sleeping figure, picked up his limp body, hoisted it over my shoulder, and teleported to Imha's castle. This time, the demons didn't advance on me. They watched me, probably wanting to attack, but knowing they weren't supposed to. Not yet.

I walked up the path, ignoring the growls and hard stares. They were only acting like that because Imha thought she was the best of all of us. If they knew how each god and goddess was exactly balanced, they wouldn't bare their teeth at me.

Corinia met me at the entrance of the castle, raised an eyebrow at the body over my shoulder, and escorted me to Imha's throne room. This time, Corinia opened the double doors but didn't go in with me. She bowed and closed the doors behind me after I entered the room. Imha was seated on her throne, playing with a purple orb.

The orb puffed out of existence and Imha stood. "A gift for me?"

"Yes." I dropped Aruhi's body at her feet.

She squealed like a child with a new toy. "I already heard about your deed. Well done."

"And?"

She strolled toward me, swished her hips. "With what you did today, how can I doubt you?" She halted in front of me. Her eyes sparkled with more than evilness. She licked her lips and rested a hand on my chest. "Besides, who says I want to doubt you?"

I refrained from stepping back. "Where's Omi?"

She shrugged. "Who cares?" She stood on her tiptoes and offered me a naughty grin. "I just got myself a new toy," she whispered.

I tried not to, but I stepped back. I turned to Aruhi. "What do you want to do with him?"

Her smile changed to a crazy one. "So many ideas."

"I could take him to your dungeon and torture him."

The shine in her eyes grew brighter. "Only if I can watch."

"I wouldn't want it any other way," I said, trying as hard as I could not to grit my teeth.

She let out a laugh like an evil queen from a fairy tale.

———

I walked out of the cell and the door slammed closed.

"Well done," Imha purred, handing me a damp rag.

I didn't say anything as I took it and wiped the blood off my hands.

She circled me, watching me with her too-clever, too-crazed eyes. "This torture session was extraordinary. I knew you still had it in you."

I forced my lips to curl up. "It was good to use my skills again."

Her smile widened. "I know. I felt it."

All I wanted to do was to get away from her. I wanted to go to my new chambers and hide there until she evaporated into nothingness.

"I think I need a shower," I said, turning toward the stairs that led out of this dark, damp dungeon.

She touched my shoulder and I fought the urge to wince. "Hmm, do you want some company?"

I glanced over my shoulder, unsure what lie I would tell her to keep her away, but as I opened my mouth, my eyes spotted something behind her and I halted. "What's that?"

A heavy wooden door stood at the other end of the corridor, symbols drawn with what looked like dried blood smeared on its surface.

"Oh, you don't know?" She bounced to the door and spied over the tiny cutout square on the top part of the door. "Come take a look."

Wary, I walked to the door and spied through the tiny window.

Oh, shit.

24

NADINE

I KNELT BEFORE TWO TOMBSTONES, ONE OF WHICH WAS MY DEAR sister's and the other the man she had married. They had lived a long life, but as with any mortal life, they eventually died.

A tear trickled down my cheek. "You stupid, stupid woman," I whispered. "You could be here with me. We could have lived together forever."

There was only me now.

And I was tired of being alone.

I looked down at my hands and blinked hard to see what lay there.

A Black Thorn.

I sat up in my bed, breathing hard.

What the hell?

One more dream about the mysterious woman. I was starting to wonder if it meant something, like the visions I used to have about the gods. Maybe these dreams were like the visions? Or maybe it was my overactive subconscious. At least I wasn't having nightmares about my family and Morgan. Well, I hadn't had any nightmares about Morgan since Micah told me he had forgiven me. Knowing he was well in the underworld also helped.

The clock on my wristwatch read a little past five in the morning. I sighed, knowing I wouldn't be able to get any more sleep. I slipped out of my sweatpants and tee, and put on some workout clothes. Maybe I could tire myself and then take a quick hot shower and go back to bed, otherwise it would be a long and tiring day.

I sighed, seeing this new pattern in my days.

As I walked into the living room, I halted. "Aren't you up a little early?" Victor and Ceris turned to me, their eyes concerned. "What is it?"

"Sit down," Ceris said.

Uh-oh, this didn't sound good.

I crossed my arms and stuffed my chest. The hell I would sit down. "What is it?"

Ceris looked to Victor and he sighed, coming to stand beside her.

Double uh-oh.

"A scout just left with an urgent message," Victor said, his voice solemn.

"What is it?"

"There's no easy way to say it," Ceris muttered. "Mitrus was behind an attack on a small Italian town."

I sucked in a sharp breath.

No, no, no, no. Micah. The Micah that had held me in my sleep. The Micah that had made breakfast for me. The Micah that had taken me to the underworld to see my family—he wouldn't do this. He couldn't.

"H-how bad was it?" My voice broke and I felt the tears coming.

"No one survived," Ceris whispered.

My knees gave in and I sat down. "When was it?"

"Last evening," Ceris said. "And he took Aruhi to Imha too."

"Aruhi?" I asked, confused.

"Sorry, I forget you don't know everyone," Ceris said. "Aruhi is a lesser god under my power." She clasped her hands together so tight her knuckles were white. "Our spy says he tortured Aruhi in front of Imha." Even she sounded sad.

Bile rose in my throat. Oh my God.

"So he's really on her side?" I asked, my voice small and weak, but I already knew the answer.

"I'm afraid so," Victor said.

Hearing that out loud hurt more than I thought it would.

"I'm sorry, Nadine," Ceris said. "I swear I wanted to believe I was wrong about him. But I wasn't. He really is on Imha's and Omi's side."

Victor reached for me. "Are you okay?"

Taking a long breath, I stood before he could touch me. "I will be."

I wiped away the tears. I wouldn't cry. I had cried too much for him already, for everyone, and I was done crying. Instead, I marched past them and hopped on the treadmill. I had some extra energy and rage to burn.

I looked out the window, gazing at nothing but the darkness, focusing on that and the black clouds surrounding us, when a tiny dark spec, even darker than the background, cut through my line of sight.

Rok.

Micah had gone but his raven had stayed.

Could the bird have stayed to watch over us, to spy on us,

or … could Rok have stayed to watch over me? I shook my head, reprimanding myself for being so naïve and stupid and dreaming that Micah cared about me.

He didn't. Otherwise he wouldn't have gone and I wouldn't feel like my heart was in pieces.

25

MICAH

"I'm not sure how long I can endure it."

"I know, my lord, but you must," Morgan said, trying to sound cheerful.

I shuddered. Imha had been nothing less than disgusting since I returned to her side. Well, pretended to have returned to her side.

She cornered me every opportunity she had, and it was never easy coming up with excuses why we couldn't jump into bed and have some fun. I shuddered again. By the Everlast. Once upon a time, I wouldn't have refused. Hell, I had initiated several of our long hours in bed. Once upon a time, I thought her craziness was exciting, intriguing, arousing. Her laugh and the evil shine in her eyes contagious.

That was centuries ago.

Now her maniacal laughter and the wicked gleam in her eyes made me want to run in the other direction.

"One of these days, she'll notice," I said. "She'll figure out that it sickens me to be near her."

"Let's hope you find out something useful before then, my lord."

I had found out several things we could use against her, but all of them would point back to me. I had to be careful what to act on. I needed something good, something big, something that wouldn't leave room for error. Something that would destroy Imha.

I hoped that something came up soon.

"I saw Nadine's family this morning, my lord," Morgan said.

"And?"

"They are well. Of course, they miss Nadine, but they are happy she's alive and well."

"Not for long," I whispered.

They wouldn't be happy to know she was trading her life for theirs, but I couldn't do anything about that now. She had made her decision. The Soul Oath was made.

I sighed and paced in front of the bar, returning my mind to the current situation.

"You'll make a hole in the floor, my lord," Morgan said.

"He's late."

"I know, my lord, but ruining your expensive floors won't fix it."

Why was he worried about the floors?

I shook my head and stopped by the bar. If I was going to have to wait, then I better wait with booze. Two doses of whiskey swallowed in five seconds.

"I'm here." Levi's voice filled the room as I was serving myself another double shot. I dropped the glass and turned to him. "Sorry, I'm late. It wasn't easy to dodge Ceris."

I gestured to the hundreds of bottles behind me. "Can I get you anything to drink?"

"I don't want—" Levi's gaze fell on Morgan and his eyes widened. "Morgan! You're here!"

Morgan bowed. "Yes, my lord. It's good to see you."

Levi offered him a small smile. "You too."

"I'm sorry, my lord, for all the problems I caused when I was under the Crimson Dagger's influence."

"It's okay, Morgan. I know you weren't yourself." Then Levi turned to me. He crossed his arms, his brows creased. "I don't have too much time, Mitrus. Tell me why you would risk our cover by calling me here."

"I can't take it anymore!" I yelled, clenching my fists. "Imha is ... ugh, she's so clingy, and it has been hard to dodge her."

"I know, brother."

"And there's Omi too. I don't think he trusts me. I think he's suspicious."

"As long as he doesn't find anything to incriminate you, it should be okay."

"But it isn't okay." I sank down on the chaise lounge. "Being there, working with them ... it disgusts me."

One side of Levi's lips curled up. "I'm glad to know that."

I growled at him. "I'm serious. I'm gonna break soon."

Levi sighed. "It was your idea, brother. Hang in there. We're almost done with all this madness. Just a few more days."

"Days?" I scoffed. "I think you mean weeks. Months."

Levi shook his head. "I hope not. I'm tired of this war. I want it to end soon."

Me too. Gods, how I wanted it to end. And yet, I didn't. Because once it was done, once the war was over, the Soul Oath would be complete, and I ... I just couldn't think about that right now.

I let out a long breath. "There's one more thing."

Levi lifted one eyebrow. "What?"

"Besides Aruhi, there's someone else in Imha's dungeons."

Noticing my dejected tone, Levi sat on the chaise across from mine. "Who?"

———

EVERY SO OFTEN, I THOUGHT ABOUT THE LIBRARY AT THE monastery. I relived the events, thinking, studying what I could have done differently. I could have gotten the Cup of Life. I could have grabbed a few books before the place burned down. I could have done so many things differently. If I had, I wouldn't have to pretend to be one of Imha's faithful minions right now. I wouldn't have to endure her evil smiles. Worse than those, her naughty smiles. I shuddered, disgusted just thinking about it.

Morgan paced in front of me.

"You're making me nervous, Morgan," I said from the chaise lounge.

He halted. "Sorry, my lord. It's just … I'm thinking."

I wasn't in the mood for talking, but I indulged him. After all, he indulged me all the time. "About?"

He looked at me with big eyes, as if he was going to tell me the discovery of the century. "What if the books survived the fire?"

"That's … how would they have survived the fire?"

He shrugged. "I don't know, my lord. I'm just pondering. I mean, that place was hidden and sacred. Surely, whoever created that place must have protected its contents against any damage. No? I don't know. I'm just rambling nonsense now."

Nonsense. But what if it wasn't? What if he was right? What if …

I stood in a flash, startling Morgan.

"You put an itch in my mind and now I'll have to go back and check it out."

Morgan wrinkled his nose. "I-I'm sorry?"

With a half-smile, I shook my head and teleported to outside the monastery. From there, I followed the same steps Levi and I had taken before but halted when I saw the library building destroyed by the fire. The fire was long gone, but the walls were black, the windows broken, and the roof had caved in.

"Shit," I muttered. I hoped I could get to the secret staircase.

It wasn't as hard as I thought it would be. The hardest part was descending the narrow staircase with all the rubble on the steps. I had to use magic several times to move aside stones and bricks.

When I finally reached the secret library, I gasped.

The walls were black, the shelves were burned to a crisp, most had fallen over or turned into ashes … but the books? The books were intact. The books and the scrolls. All of them. Perfectly intact.

"No way."

Morgan had been right! There was a spell on the library's contents.

In haste, I moved over the shelves—most crumbled into even smaller pieces when I tried to lift them—and went back to the last place I had seen the book. Under a broken shelf and more books, I found it. The book about Diana. I opened it and made sure the pages were all still there. Not ripped out, not burned.

Incredible.

I teleported back to my lair in the underworld.

"Back already?" Morgan asked, his brow at his hairline. His eyes found the book in my hands. "There was a spell on the books?"

"It seems that way." I sat down on the chaise and flipped the book open to the chapter about the ladies of Diana. "Here."

Morgan leaned over my shoulder and read it with me.

The ladies of Diana were females who had been chosen to serve Diana, helping her maintain justice and peace in the world.

Often ladies of Diana were confused with heroes from the Everlasting Circle. However, heroes were chosen by the Fates, while the ladies of Diana were chosen by Diana's magic. Another difference is heroes were stronger and had an accelerated healing, while ladies of Diana were stronger, had accelerated healing, but also had special abilities.

Most ladies of Diana possessed several abilities, like being expert warriors with any kind of weapon, being able to heal minor injuries or pains from humans and lesser gods, and finding missing people. These special abilities varied from lady to lady, depending mostly on their ranking under Diana's command.

"That's it," Morgan said, his voice full of wonder. "Nadine is a lady of Diana. That's why she could heal you and Lord Levi. That's why she found the scepters and is now finding other gods. And I'm guessing Alice is one too."

And Keisha was one too.

That made sense.

I handed the book to Morgan and started pacing. Morgan sat down with the book open and he became immersed in it.

Meanwhile, I let my mind wander, remembering each of the times Nadine had touched me and healed me, the time she had found Levi's and my scepters, and then given us the energy to transform into full gods. The times she had looked at the map and seen symbols, even when no one else could see them. And she had become an expert fighter in such a short time.

It did make sense.

But why didn't her aura read like Alice's and Keisha's? Every god or goddess knew what Alice and Keisha were from their auras, but we didn't feel the same thing with Nadine's. Why?

"I think I may have found something, my lord," Morgan announced.

I turned to him. "Yes?"

Morgan turned the book to me. "See this chapter?" He pointed to the picture of Diana. She stood in front of her ladies, holding a crystal spear. "This chapter talks about Diana's weapon, the spear of justice. According to this text, the spear has a unique power. It can render any enemy immobile, even major gods, allowing Diana to pass judgment without any interference."

I frowned. "This Diana is powerful, huh?"

"She was."

If Diana could really render any enemy immobile, she could win this entire freaking war for us. "We should look for her. She could be of great help."

"My lord, there's another chapter here that explains more about Diana's vanishing act. It says that she's not just hiding. It says she's dead. For real. Otherwise, don't you think she would have stopped Lady Imha and Lord Omi by now? She is the goddess of justice, after all."

By the Everlast, I wished he weren't right. If Diana was still around, she could be a great ally. Our ultimate weapon. But if she was alive and hiding, then she had some explaining to do.

"How about her spear?" I asked.

Morgan narrowed his eyes. "What about it?"

"Maybe we can't find Diana, but we can try to find her spear, and with the spear, we can stop Imha and Omi."

"That's a good theory."

I clicked my tongue, realizing something important. "To activate our scepters, we had to be the ones to hold it. If this spear is like that, we won't be able to touch it."

"Maybe you can't, but the ladies of Diana can."

"Nadine," I whispered.

"Or Alice," Morgan offered.

"Yeah, right. Her too." He smiled. "I should tell the others." I was ready to teleport to NYC, but Morgan raised his hand.

"You shouldn't go, my lord. Your cover might be blown if you do."

Damn it. "I'll send a message to Levi, then."

ALICE AND I WALKED OUT OF THE GYM AND SAW VICTOR AT THE door, accepting a rolled paper from a man I had never seen before.

I stopped and watched as Victor nodded to the man, then closed the door, his eyes on the rolled paper in his hands. Uninterested, Alice went to the kitchen.

I wiped the sweat from my face with my towel. "Who was that?"

He looked up from the paper. "I'm not entirely sure," he said, his voice low, distant.

He unrolled the paper and read it. His forehead creased and his lips pressed into a thin line. Not good.

Finally, he rolled the paper and beckoned me to follow him. Wary, I went with him to his bedroom, where Ceris was seated in an armchair reading a book about the creed. She closed the book and raised her eyebrows at us. At the little table beside her, a wild rose-scented candle burned.

He marched to the bed, sat on the mattress, and swept his

hand in front of him. The map I had left in my bedroom appeared on the mattress.

"I need you to find someone for me," he said.

I walked to the bed and looked down at the map. "Who?"

He extended his hand between us and a bolt of white power appeared floating over his palm. The bolt morphed into a symbol. A round circle, like the other gods and goddesses, with lines of varying width crossing each other in the center.

"Find this symbol. Please."

I sat down beside him and focused on the map. The symbols sprouted to life, their white shine blinking all over the map. I still hadn't figured out what that meant. Were these deities teleporting like Ceris did every time we left our apartment, or was their energy lost and spread throughout the world?

Ceris stood from the armchair and sat on the other side of the bed. "Whose symbol is that?"

Victor lifted one finger, as if asking her for a moment. "Do you see it?"

I focused on the map. It didn't matter who it was, as long as we could find him or her, and convince this deity to join us. Our time to assemble an army was running out.

I searched for over twenty minutes, while Ceris and Victor breathed down my neck, waiting and making me tense.

"I don't see anything," I finally said. "Maybe this deity is hiding his aura."

Victor shook his head. "I think this deity is dead. I wanted to find her weapon."

"Why?" Ceris asked.

Victor looked at the paper rolled in his hand. "It doesn't matter now."

Ceris pointed to the paper. "What is that?"

Victor waved his hand and the paper disappeared. "Nothing."

Ceris glared at him but didn't say anything.

Meanwhile, I continued staring at the map. If the deity were dead, I couldn't find her, but if her weapon was still around, I should be able to find it, just as I had found Victor's and Micah's scepters.

I closed my eyes and took a deep breath, emptying my mind. Feeling silly, I called on the magic, whatever magic was hidden in me—if any. I opened my eyes and concentrated on the map. I searched each millimeter, ignoring the blinking and moving symbols I saw all the time. They weren't the ones I was looking for.

Then I saw it. A faint little thing, hidden under several of the blinking, moving symbols. It never moved or blinked, and with the other symbols jumping around it, its shine became almost imperceptible. Almost.

"I found it," I said.

Victor stiffened. "You did?" I nodded and he rushed to my side, leaning over the map. "Where is it?"

I pointed to the Coliseum in Rome.

Ceris crossed her arms. "All right, now tell us. Who is this deity?"

Victor sighed. "A long time ago, there was a goddess who ruled separately from the Everlasting Circle, but adjacent. Her name was Diana, the goddess of justice, courage, wisdom, and honesty. She could overrule us."

Ceris's brows dipped into a frown. "Wait, I don't remember any goddess named Diana."

"Like I said, it was too long ago. We forgot about her."

"But ... how did we forget her?" Ceris asked.

"That doesn't matter," Victor answered. "What matters is that Nadine may have found Diana's spear."

"What is so special about that spear?" I asked.

Victor stood from the bed and looked at us, a revived shine in his blue-green eyes. "As the goddess of justice, Diana had the power to pass judgment over us, and her spear had the ability to render any deity immobile while doing it."

Ceris gasped. "So, with the spear we can capture Imha and Omi."

The corners of Victor's lips tugged up and he nodded. "Exactly."

"But if this spear is like your scepters, only you can use it," I pointed out. "And this Diana is dead."

"Well, this is where the next bit of information comes in," Victor said. Now he sounded like a crazy scientist going over his incredible finding. "I have reason to believe Alice isn't a hero."

I frowned. "Then what is she?"

He smiled. "The same thing you are."

"W-what?"

"Along with Diana, there was a group of females called the ladies of Diana. These females were accomplished warriors, much like heroes, who helped Diana with her duties. They rose in rank and the highest-ranking lady was known for several abilities. Finding deities, minor healing, a little magic ..."

I gasped.

"Nadine and Alice are ladies of Diana," Ceris whispered with wide eyes.

"And Keisha was one too," Victor added.

"But ..." I couldn't find any words for this new discovery.

"It makes sense," Victor said. "Look at everything you did, everything you can do. It's not a coincidence. We knew you were something. Now we know what."

I stood. "That's ... impossible."

"Why?" Victor asked. "By now, you should have realized nothing is impossible."

I did realize that, but this was different. This was me, my life. It was one thing to think, to presume, there was magic in me, and another to know there was magic in me and to know where it came from.

Lady of Diana. And not just any lady. Judging by the many abilities I possessed, a high-ranked one.

"I think Nadine can take and use the spear," Victor continued, adding to my shock. "As Diana's highest-ranked lady among us, you should be able to."

"But ... what if this is all a mistake?" I asked. "I mean, what if we're not ladies of Diana. What if we're something else?"

Victor sighed. "If you aren't a lady of Diana, then we'll know when you try to take the spear and can't."

I swallowed. I was trying to reason against gods. Better to just do whatever they were telling me. If they were right, good. If they were wrong, we could scratch this and focus on another theory.

"All right." I filled my lungs with air as if it could provide me with courage. "When are we leaving?"

"Not we. Just you," Victor said.

"What?" Ceris asked, her blue eyes hard on him. "Levi, can I talk to you for a minute?" She walked to the other side of the bedroom.

With a heavy sigh, Victor stood and walked to her. They

exchanged a few harsh whispers while I pretended I wasn't seeing anything.

After two minutes, Ceris walked out of the bedroom and Victor turned to me. "Go gear up and pack. You're leaving now."

I opened my mouth to ask more questions about it— What did he mean leave now? Where was I going? How would I find the spear by myself? And if I ran into a band of demons? Or Imha? But his cold eyes told me not to question it. Not now.

I swallowed my protests and marched to my bedroom.

I put on our beige armor and boots, packed a small leather satchel with an extra change of clothes and some food and water, grabbed a sword and two small daggers from the training room. All the while trying to ignore the nervousness rising in me.

Oh my God, that was what I was? A lady of Diana? We had finally found out? How had Victor stumbled on this information? He didn't just find it this morning, lying around our living room.

When I was ready, Victor escorted me out of the building —quietly, almost as if he didn't want anyone else to see me.

"You have four days to find the spear and come back. On the fifth day, we'll have all of our allies gathered here, and we'll march on Imha."

Four days. If I didn't have someone to teleport me, I wasn't sure how to get there and come back in four days. I still couldn't believe he was sending me away. How the hell was I supposed to cross the ocean alone in four days? Make that two days since I had to go and come back.

"Are you giving me any details, or I'm supposed to figure out what to do and how to get there by myself?"

"You won't be alone," Victor said as we crossed the protective shield. He touched my arm and teleported us to three random places before arriving at what looked like an deserted road in Japan—that was what I assumed by the looks of the abandoned buildings along the road.

With a frown, I looked around. "So?"

A new form flashed in front of us. My heart lurched and I took a step back.

"Hi, darling," Micah said. His face was serious though, without his usual confident smirk.

I raised my sword, ready to defend myself, but Victor closed his hand around my arm. "It's fine," he said. "Mitrus is on our side."

I gaped. "W-what?"

"He's our main spy inside Imha's army."

I looked at Micah. But ... "The town. Those lives. What about Aruhi?"

"An illusion," Micah said, his black eyes on mine. "Aruhi helped me evacuate the town before we burned it, and then he used his magic to make it look like everyone was still there. As for him, he volunteered to be captured and taken to Imha. I didn't like the idea, but I was able to convince Imha to let me handle his torture sessions, which are another illusion."

"This way, she can't doubt Mitrus," Victor explained. "She really trusts he is on her side."

On her side ...

Nausea rolled in my stomach. Nausea and rage. Oh my God, he let me believe he was on her side. That he was helping her and killing innocents.

Without thinking, I advanced on him and punched his

shoulder. "Do you have any idea how sick I was, thinking you had turned on us?"

"Ow." He stepped back, getting away from me before I punched him again. "I'm sorry, but it had to be this way."

I glanced from Micah to Victor. "So, that fight and argument was for show?"

Micah and Victor exchanged a tight glance.

"Yes," Micah answered. "On our last mission together, Levi and I found out we have a real spy in our midst. So, we decided Imha should have one too."

"We already have one spy inside Imha's army," I said, my voice low. "One of the scouts volunteered for that."

Victor nodded. "Yes, but as a regular deity, he will never rise in rank or know everything she's plotting."

"And you do?" I asked, watching Micah, trying to see through all the layers he had raised around himself.

He stared at me, not answering. My heart plummeted. What did his damn silence mean? He was close to her? He was with her? I wasn't sure whether I should feel disgusted or relieved.

Victor spoke up. "Thanks to him, we now have every reason to believe we're ahead of Imha."

Micah offered me his hand. "Ready to go?"

I stared at his hand. "You're going with me?"

He nodded.

"Mitrus was the one who found out about Diana and her ladies," Victor said.

Micah shook his head. "You helped, Levi. And Morgan too."

"Morgan deserves a big reward," Victor said. "Now, you two better get going. You have four days. Only four days."

"Don't worry," Micah said. "We'll be back before that." He turned to me. "Are you ready?"

Ready to go away alone with Micah to find a spear that would change everything? Not really.

Victor put a hand on my shoulder. "Be careful. Both of you."

Micah shrugged it off as if we were going for a stroll on the park. He extended his hand to me again. Oh, God. To teleport with him, we had to touch. This quest, this mission, would be awkward.

I inhaled and took his hand. "I'm ready."

27

NADINE

LIKE CERIS USUALLY DID, MICAH POPPED US TO RANDOM PLACES before stopping in a narrow alley. Immediately, I stepped away from him, lowering my hand from his. "Where are we?"

I spied around the corner. We were on a quiet and dark street, flanked by commercial buildings with too many metal bars on the windows and doors. Lamps were broken, sidewalks were littered, and the few people walking around looked drunk or starving.

"A stop we need to make." A black leather jacket appeared in his hand. He quickly wrapped it around me. "Put that on and stay close."

Micah stepped out of the alley. He turned to the building on our left. A broken wooden sign hung above the secured door. Al's Pub.

"A pub?" I asked, but he didn't acknowledge me. I shoved my arms through the sleeves of the leather jacket.

Micah knocked on the closed door. A large guy with a long beard opened the inside door, keeping the metal bars between us.

"Can I help you?" the guy asked.

"We would like a drink," Micah said. The guy looked over us. He didn't seem too amused by Micah, but his eyes hovered over me from my head to toe. I stifled a shudder. With a big frown, Micah pulled a few bills from his pocket and passed it on to the guy. "To help you decide."

The guy took the cash and pocketed it, then unlocked the metal bar door. "Come in." He stepped aside.

Micah closed his hand around my lower arm and guided me in front of him. He pushed me inside the pub—a tiny, rustic thing with a dozen or so customers sitting at the low, wooden tables, and another four or five drinking at the bar— and to a table in a corner.

He pulled out a chair for me. I thought about being stubborn and taking another, but I didn't want to appear childish, so I sat down. He took the chair across from me, his eyes on the front door.

"Are you going to tell me what we are doing here, or am I supposed to be a good worshiper and just be quiet?"

He looked at me. "I need to meet someone before we look for the spear."

"We're wasting time."

"Hopefully not much."

"Then let's not waste any time and let's go." The sooner we found the spear, the sooner I would be rid of him.

"Do you think it's easy to disappear from Imha for four days?"

I frowned. "What does that have to do with my quest?"

"The person we're meeting will help me with that."

Oh.

A fake blond waitress with too much cleavage and not

much underneath it to show leaned over the table, batting her lashes at Micah. "Hi, handsome. What can I get you?"

He stared right into her eyes as if gazing into her cleavage wasn't even an option. "A soda for the lady, and a beer for me."

She snapped her head, looking at me, and her eyes widened. What? She hadn't seen me here? Guess with a guy like Micah around it was hard to notice anything else.

She humphed then sashayed back to the bar.

I crossed my arms and looked everywhere but at him. I didn't know what to say or how to act. I was still mad at him for all he had done, for all he had let me believe he had done.

The waitress came back. She threw the soda my way—and almost dumped it all over me—then leaned closer to Micah. "Here you go, handsome." She handed him his beer.

Without looking at her, Micah took the beer. "Thank you."

"Anything else?"

"No, we are good."

Reluctantly, the waitress walked away.

The silence and the tension were killing me. I might be mad at him, but I was also curious.

"So, having too much fun with Imha?"

He frowned. "Having too much fun with Ceris?"

Touché.

"You know, Ceris can behave. Sometimes." I doubted we would ever go back to being Cheryl and me, but I believed I could handle her until the war was over.

"I wish I could say the same of Imha," he muttered.

"Why are you doing this?" I asked.

He looked at me, head tilted. "Doing what?"

"Two things." I lifted my index finger. "One, why are you working as a spy?"

He sighed. "Because things weren't going so great when I was working with you and the others. I couldn't prove my worth, and I was blamed for every little mess. Not saying I was innocent, but even if I was responsible for them, it wasn't my intention. Even Levi started doubting my worth. And then we started suspecting we have an actual spy among us." His eyes were too intense, too truthful. I averted my gaze. "I knew I could gain Imha's trust again and having someone close to her is, in my opinion, the best way to defeat her."

I wanted to ask more. I wanted to know if she was hitting on him. If to remain in character, he was conceding to her *every* wish. Or maybe he wanted to. Maybe he didn't mind having her all over him.

I shuddered.

I lifted my middle finger. "Two, why are you helping me?"

"Someone has to."

Ouch. I guess I saw that coming, but for some reason I hoped the answer would be different.

I leaned back in the chair and sipped my soda in silence.

Soon, Micah stiffened, his eyes on the front door.

A man entered the pub, and after looking around, he marched to our table. He sat on the chair by my side.

"Have you figured out what to do?" Micah asked.

"Yes, but I'll need your blood," the guy answered.

Promptly, Micah dropped his arm on the table and rolled his sleeve up. He fished a dagger from his waist and—

"Whoa," I said.

—slashed a thin cut on his lower arm. The guy took a small flask from his pocket and held it beside the cut. Micah squeezed the cut, guiding the blood inside the vial.

"What else?"

"I can get the rest." The man closed the vial and returned it to his pocket.

Micah grabbed a napkin and wiped the cut on his arm. "And Aruhi?"

"I'll need his blood too."

He rolled his sleeves back down. "Can you get to him?"

"Maybe, if I can keep Imha distracted."

"Do whatever you have to do," Micah said. Nodding, the man stood. "Thank you."

"My pleasure, my lord." The man lowered his head in a tiny bow, and then left the pub in a hurry.

I waited until he was gone and the doors closed behind him before turning to Micah. "What the hell was that?"

Micah sighed. "That's the other spy we have working inside Imha's army, the former scout, but he doesn't have the access I have. Anyway, he'll create an illusion of me destroying another empty town and torturing the towns-people so Imha thinks I'm busy."

How many of these people could play with illusions? "And Aruhi?"

"He will create another illusion for Aruhi so he appears beaten and weak. Hopefully, Imha will be too busy with other things and forget about Aruhi."

Wow, I was impressed. He really thought of everything for this.

In a long swallow, Micah finished his beer and slapped the empty glass on the table. "So, are you ready to go?"

I took two more sips of my soda and nodded.

Side by side, we walked back to the alley. I extended my hand to him before he could ask for it. I swear one corner of his lips curled up as he caught my hand in his and teleported us out of there.

After a few more stops, he let go of my hand.

I looked around. A dense forest. Tall trees, yellowish grass. The smell of recent rain.

"I know this place," I said.

Without a word, Micah walked through the trees and I followed him. Soon, the trees gave way to a clearing, and in the center of the clearing stood the Fates' cottage. Rok appeared among the trees and flew around the little house. How was it that he could simply appear wherever he wanted? I mean, he didn't just fly from New York to ... wherever the Fates' cottage was.

"What are we doing here? I thought we were going to find the spear."

"We will, but it's late and I'm tired. I'm guessing that finding the spear won't be quick or easy, so I would rather stop now. We need to rest before proceeding. Only the Everlast Energy knows how long it'll take us to find the spear."

"And the Fates' place is the best you could come up with?"

"Not really, but they aren't here, and they don't mind us using it to hide from Imha and Omi."

God, I hoped they didn't find us here.

We walked in the cottage. I had never been here, not physically. Only in my visions.

Micah pointed to a door on the other side of the small living room. "The bedrooms and bathroom are through there." Then he pointed to a door on our left. "And there's the kitchen, in case you're hungry."

I walked to the farthest door and looked inside. A short hallway, three small bedrooms, and a bathroom—too similar to the cottage on the Croatian island.

"Is there a specific room I should take?"

He shook his head. "Any room."

"All right." I reached up and twirled a strand of my hair in my finger. This time, I was certain one corner of his lips curled up. By a millimeter, but it did. "Good night."

"Good night, Nadine."

I walked into one of the bedrooms and closed the door behind me.

———

THE SAME NIGHTMARE THAT WOKE ME UP ALMOST EVERY NIGHT visited me. The girl and me, and then flames consuming my family. It wasn't even five in the morning when I sat up in bed, breathing hard.

At first, I didn't recognize where I was and panic made its way through my chest. Then everything came rushing through my mind and I remembered. I was at the Fates' cottage. In the middle of nowhere. Alone with Micah.

I stared at the closed door. He was sleeping in one of the other rooms, just outside this door. Probably wearing only sweatpants or something similar. With his ripped chest bare. I shook my head, ashamed for still having too many strong feelings for him. After all he had done, all he had put me through, I still couldn't *not* like him. It was stupid.

Muttering curses to myself, I put on the rest of my gear—I hadn't taken it all off last night, and since I had packed light and hadn't brought pajamas, I had slept in my uniform pants and a thermal tee.

I pulled my hair into a ponytail, finished packing the little stuff I brought, slung the strap of my backpack on my shoulders, and walked out of the room. Just as Micah was walking out of his, his hair disheveled and his chest bare. I froze at the door, staring at him and his perfection with only black sweat-pants—just like I had imagined. Actually, my imagination could only go so far. The real thing was even more ripped than the guy in my dreams.

God, it wasn't fair. It really, really wasn't fair to my poor heart.

He had a new, intricate tattoo. It was a black, thick web originating from his heart and reaching to his shoulder and stomach. It covered some of his old tattoos and didn't really make sense to me, but I refused to ask him about it. Or why the hell he got a new tattoo when we were at war.

"Morning, darling," he said, already sounding way too chirpy for five in the morning.

I grunted and walked past him, going to the kitchen. I got busy making a quick breakfast and packing a lunch and some snacks—who knew when we would find food again? Right, Micah could teleport any time he wanted, but what if we got into a situation where he couldn't? Anyway, I wasn't taking any chances.

A few minutes later, Micah joined me in the kitchen. He had a fresh face as if he had showered. As usual, he wore all black. I wondered why he wasn't wearing his gear, like me, but I decided not to ask. The less I talked to him the better.

"Were you planning on waking up at five in the morning, or did I wake you up?" I asked, not doing too well on my promise to stay quiet.

"Actually, I heard you screaming earlier."

I gaped at him. "I was screaming again?"

He nodded. "And that pain? No sign of it?"

"No," I said. "Sorry about waking you up with my screams."

He shrugged. "It's okay." He took two large steps and stood beside me, looking around the table, where all the food was already packed. "I could have helped with this."

"It's fine."

We reached for the same pack of snacks, and I withdrew my hand. He grabbed it before I could pull away.

"Darling, I—"

"Do *not* call me that," I said through gritted teeth. I stepped back, taking my hand with me.

"But I want to—"

"Whatever you have to say, I don't want to hear." I took another step back. "Please, don't make this worse than it already is. Let's ... just get this over with."

I zipped my backpack and walked out of the kitchen, and out of the cottage. Outside, I leaned against the wall, my heart beating fast and my hand—the one he had touched—cradled against my chest. A zing had run through me when his skin had met mine. God, I hated this. I hated how it was agonizing to be around him. To be right beside him.

I closed my eyes, took a deep breath, and slowed my heart rate. When Micah walked out of the cottage a few minutes later, I was ready to go on this damn quest.

Until he extended his hand to me. "I can teleport us there." I stared at his hand. "Unless you prefer doing it the hard way. Stolen cars, broken trains, maybe a ship or two, and lots of walking. And even so, we won't get there in the next three months."

Damn, he was right. Suppressing a groan, I rested my hand in his, ignoring the way his big, warm hand enveloped mine like they were pieces of the same puzzle.

"Here we go," he said.

Three seconds later, we were in the middle of nowhere,

with hills all around us. Rok flew ahead, disappearing on the dark horizon.

"Where are we?"

"Just outside Rome," he said, looking around. There was a broken road about one hundred yards from us and it stretched out until it disappeared among the hills. "I tried teleporting to the outside of the Coliseum, but I can't. There's a barrier around the city."

"That's not good."

He shook his head, watching the road. "No, it's not. But we've got no option. If we follow this road, we should arrive in Rome." He started walking toward the road. "Come on."

I rushed to follow him. With his big steps, he walked much faster than I did.

After a few minutes of walking in silence, I asked, "Didn't Imha destroy Rome a few months ago?"

"Yes."

"Then, isn't the Coliseum destroyed too? I mean more destroyed than it already was before the attack."

"I don't know." He glanced at me. "Let's hope it isn't."

We walked for hours, until finally we saw the city opening up before us—all ruins. The roads and bridges broken, the buildings and houses crumbled to the ground.

As we stepped into the city, Micah took a sharp inhale.

"What is it?"

"We just crossed through a barrier." His expression hardened. A knot formed on his forehead and his jaw tensed. "I can sense demons all around us."

"Damn it," I whispered.

"We better hide." He grabbed my hand—again, I felt the zing—and pulled me to the debris of two fallen buildings. "We'll need to be extra careful."

We stayed in the darkness and I wondered why we weren't moving—with caution, of course. I opened my mouth to ask him when I heard it. The heavy footfall of several demons.

Micah, still holding my hand, pulled me even deeper into the debris.

"What about my aura?" I asked in a low whisper. "I know they can't sense it, but what if Imha or Omi are around?"

"I'm hiding our auras," he said simply.

I didn't see them, but I heard the demons growing closer and closer, and then getting farther and farther away.

"I don't understand," I said, once it seemed okay to talk again. "Why is there a barrier and demons in Rome?"

"Perhaps there's something here that Imha is after."

I gasped. "Do you think she knows about the ladies of Diana and the spear?"

"I don't think so. Or, at least, I hope she doesn't." He finally let go of my hand and moved to the edge of the crumbling buildings. He looked out—side to side, up and down. "It's clear. Let's go."

And just like that, he marched ahead of me as if he couldn't stand to be near me.

28

I HAD NEVER BEEN TO ROME BEFORE OR EUROPE OR EVEN outside the United States. But Micah had. Before he had come to New York City and found me, he had traveled around the world, looking for people like him, and Rome had been one of his destinations.

Even though it was hard to tell where anything was among the ruins, Micah had assured me he had a pretty good idea of where the Coliseum stood—or used to stand—so I trusted him and let him be our guide as we walked and hid from the demon patrols.

The hiding, the walking through the debris, the crossing broken bridges and roads went slowly. I had no idea how far we were from the Coliseum, but it certainly didn't look like we would arrive there today.

However, we couldn't stop for the night either. What if we let our guard down and were surprised by demons? Or Imha and Omi? No, thank you. I preferred to keep going and be done with this, even if it meant not sleeping, even if I was tired and my legs ached from walking so much—I would compensate later.

It was getting late—though with the sun hidden by endless black, there wasn't much difference between day and night anyway. We slowed down as we passed through an intact cemetery behind a burned down church. I didn't want to, but it was like there was a force pulling my eyes to look at the tombstones. I read all the names, all the dates, and little, special messages. Why had these people died? Because of Imha? Because of the darkness? Or had they died of some illness or old age?

Suddenly, Micah stopped. "Darl—um, Nadine?" he called me.

I halted beside him. "Yeah?"

"I can't sense any demons. Maybe we should rest for a bit now."

I looked around at all the tombstones. "You want to stop here? No way."

He scanned the area. "Why not?"

"You may be the god of death, but sitting around a bunch of dead people makes me uncomfortable. No way."

One corner of his lips tugged up, and I could swear I saw a bit of the old Micah, the cocky one, hiding behind the one in front of me. "All right. Let's find somewhere to sit down as soon as we're out of here."

A few minutes later, we found a small park across the street from the cemetery.

"Is this place okay?" Micah asked, his tone teasing.

I rolled my eyes and didn't answer him. Instead, I plopped down on a broken bench, crisscross applesauce style, and pulled a bottle of water and snacks from my backpack.

Micah sat down on a patch of dead grass a couple of feet from me. "Do you have any beer?"

"Of course. I have beer, scotch, tequila, and vodka. What do you want?"

He smiled. Not a full, touching-the-eyes kind of smile, but a small smile. One that made my heart pitter-patter. I didn't know what he saw in my face because he lost that beautiful smile a couple of seconds later.

He sighed. "You know, I need to tell you a few things—"

I shook my head. "Please, don't."

"But I need to. Please, darling, just listen to me."

I glared at him. There was that damned nickname again. "We're past this, Micah. You don't need to tell me anything."

"It doesn't matter. You can't run from me right now, so if I talk, you'll have to listen."

"Don't you dare."

He ignored me and commenced his speech. "I'm sorry about Keisha. I never meant to kill her. I swear I probably felt her death as much as you did." I averted my eyes because I couldn't take the intensity, the truth in his stare. It didn't lessen the pain of her death, though. "As for siding with Imha ... you know that's a facade, the only way I found to be useful after making so many mistakes. And it was better if our spy thinks Levi and I had a real argument and I left on bad terms. More importantly, I need you to know it disgusts me to be close to Imha again. It physically hurts and makes me sick. I'll never be with Imha again. Even if we really live forever, I won't be with her. I promise you that." Why was he telling me this? Did he think I cared? Did he *know* I cared? I willed my expression to be blank, careless. I failed big time. He cleared his throat. "The last thing I wanted to tell you is I volunteered to come with you on this mission because I don't trust your safety to anyone else. I wanted to be here with you."

I snapped my head back to him and saw in his dark eyes he was telling the truth. Why, gods? Why was he torturing me like this?

Pushing aside my feelings, I stood. "We should keep going."

"But we just stopped. You need to rest a little more."

"I'm fine," I said, picking up my backpack from the bench. "I don't want to rest."

I did *want* to rest. I was tired from walking all day and sleeping so little at night. I kind of needed some rest—not that I would ever tell him.

As soon as I started walking, I realized I didn't really know the direction we were heading, but I was too stubborn to stop.

"Nadine, wait," Micah called me. I heard his fast footsteps, catching up with me. I walked faster. After a few seconds, Micah's hand closed around my upper arm.

I glared at him. "Hey!"

He put a finger over his lips. "Shh. I sense demons coming this way, fast."

That shut me up.

Micah slid his hand down my arm until my hand was safe in his. He tugged my arm and pulled me back to the broken bench in the middle of the park. We looked around—there was no good place to hide, so we crouched behind the bench and prayed that it was enough.

The demons appeared from the other side of the park in an organized fashion, with four demons side by side and six rows—just like a battalion ready for battle. I shuddered, remembering the many times I had been too close to them.

They continued down a stone path across the park and

seemed not to have noticed us. Until the Akuma—the bat-like demons—swooped in the dark sky. With their bird's-eye view and their great night vision, they spotted us.

With a shriek, the Akuma swooped toward us—I counted four. The other demons—a mix of the Ornek and Arak—stopped their march and turned their attention to us.

"Fuck," Micah cursed.

29

MICAH

WE STOOD AND PULLED OUT OUR SWORDS AS THE TWENTY-eight demons rushed us. The Akuma lunged at us, their talons ready to pierce, slash, massacre. I threw my power at them, causing two to stagger and another to fall back. The other twenty-three demons surrounded us. I searched for the twenty-fourth and found him running away. No, not running away. Running to warn other demons of our presence here.

"Shit," I muttered. As fast as I could, I threw three black bolts at the demons right in front of me, making them move, and then channeled my power and sent one big, powerful bolt at the demon in the distance. The bolt hit it square in the back and he went down.

I sighed in relief for half a second before the other demons lunged at me.

Behind me, Nadine engaged the two remaining Akuma that had attacked her. I couldn't watch it, but I sneaked a few glances every few seconds to make sure she was all right, and every time I was in awe of how beautifully she moved, how deadly she held herself, how precisely she used her sword. It was incredible how she had grown as a warrior in the last few weeks.

She dispatched the two Akuma, just to have five other demons pounce on her.

"Can you feel your magic?" I yelled at her, hoping she would hear me over the growls and the sword clanks.

"What do you mean?" she asked, her tone equally high.

"Now would be a good time to use your magic, if you can."

I heard her groan. "I don't know how to call it or control it."

A demon made a swipe at my head and I ducked out of the way. Damn, too close. I created a shield in front of me to gain some time, and threw bolts at the demons on the side.

I wasn't sure since I couldn't turn around and waste time counting, but I would have guessed we were already down to half the demons we started with. Nadine and I kept on fighting, as if it was as easy and normal as breathing, until one of the Akuma that had fallen back rose in the sky, its chest singed by my previous bolt, and then dove like a bird of prey.

"Nadine!" I shouted, turning to her.

She was parrying the attack of another demon and didn't see, couldn't see, the Akuma diving at her. I pushed her out of the way, but the Akuma still got its talons deep into her shoulder. Nadine screamed but didn't stop. She jerked aside, making the Akuma release her, and sliced its claw with her sword, severing its limb. The demon let out a shrill shriek, chilling my spine. In that moment, I placed my hand on its back, right between the crown of his wings, and let out my power. The Akuma burned to a crisp in seconds.

Blood flowed from Nadine's shoulder as she killed

another two demons. I fought the urge to drop everything, run to her, and kill the last four.

Then she turned to me, her uniform ripped, her shoulder and chest bloodied, and her face pale. Her green eyes locked with mine, but I doubted she saw anything as she fell to her knees.

With my heart in my throat, I ran to her.

30

NADINE

MICAH HELPED ME SIT DOWN ON THE BENCH. "LET ME SEE," HE said, reaching for my shoulder.

"It's nothing." I raised my arm to push his hand away, but flinched from the pain radiating from the wound when I moved. I had almost fainted after the battle was over. Almost. I had felt the strength seeping out of me, and hit my knees hard on the concrete ground, making it all hurt more.

As he knelt on the ground in front of me, Micah tsked. "Darling, you're not a very good liar."

I groaned and let him pull the ripped piece of my armor aside to look at the wound. I hissed, and cursed, and hissed some more.

"Here." He offered me his left arm. "You can hold on, squeeze, dig your nails in. Do whatever, as long as you let me clean this up."

I waved him off. "I can take it."

He raised an eyebrow at me. "Okay." He ripped the cloth around the wound some more, and then grabbed supplies from my backpack—water, antiseptic, gauze, and tape. "I need to clean it first to see how bad it is." He uncapped the water bottle. "This is going to hurt."

I looked away, trying to focus on anything but the wound on my shoulder, or the fact that his face was mere inches from mine. "I'm fine. Do it."

Micah poured some water over the wound, and I suppressed a cry as the burning pain increased tenfold. Mindlessly, I reached for his arm and squeezed it.

I pretended not to see the corners of his lips tugging up.

"It's not too bad." His voice dripped with relief. "I thought the demon had gone deeper. And when I saw the blood on your chest ..." He shook his head.

"It was just a little blood from my shoulder," I said.

He sighed. "It's just an ugly scratch. You'll be fine if we clean it every few hours." He dropped the water bottle and grabbed the antiseptic. "This is going to hurt too. Ready?"

I didn't feel ready, but I nodded. Better get this over with. Not caring about wasting it, Micah poured the antiseptic over the scratch.

"Oh my God," I muttered, losing my voice to the burning pain. I squeezed his arm, digging my nails on his tee.

"Sorry, darling, but it'll get infected if we don't clean it well." He poured some more of the antiseptic, and I cursed everyone I knew and didn't know while holding on to his arm for dear life.

When the pain subsided a little, Micah open up the gauze and started taping the squares on my shoulder.

"I'm sorry," he repeated.

"It's okay. The pain is manageable now."

He shook his head. "That's not what I meant." He stopped working on my wound and looked at me. "I came on this mission to make sure you didn't get hurt. And here you are. Hurt."

I watched him. The heavy set of his brows, the sharp lines of his jaw and chin and cheekbones, the fullness of his lips, the perfect line of his nose, and his black eyes—his eyes that revealed too much. Dread, worry, relief, caring.

A sharp pang cut through my heart. "It wasn't your fault. And, regardless of any injuries, I'm …" I paused and took a deep breath. "I'm glad you're here with me."

Surprise registered in his eyes, but only for a second before being replaced by hunger, by wanting. The hand working on the scratch slid to my neck and cupped my face as he stretched his frame, leaning over me. I didn't think. I just met him halfway. His lips touched mine and I let out a sigh. My lips parted, molding to his and allowing him free pass. His tongue teased mine as if he was afraid that if he pushed too far, I would pull away.

And I should. Pull away. Right now.

This instant.

But I couldn't. I was too drunk on him to do anything else other than take more. Ask for more.

I spread my legs open and Micah scooted between them, coming closer. He wound one of his arms around my waist and pressed on my back, bringing my chest to his. He shifted his weight, aligning his hips with mine, and I could feel how much he wanted me. Letting my hormones and feelings speak louder, I just acted. I held on to his shoulders and ground my hips against his. He groaned and nipped at my lower lip. I moved against him again and this time he cursed under his breath. Slowly, his lips slid down my neck, leaving a searing mark whenever they touched me. He ran his hand up my arm and over my shoulder.

I gasped as a shock of pain spread from my shoulder, down my arm, to my fingertips.

Micah pulled away immediately. "Fuck, I forgot about your scratch." He rested his hands over my knees. "Did I hurt you?"

I just stared at him, too shocked to reply. How did I let this happen? One second we were being attacked, the next we were kissing? When and why did I let my guard down? It didn't make any sense. I knew better than this.

"No, um, I just felt it when you touched it." I reached for my backpack on the ground.

"I'm sorry, darling. I—"

"It's okay." I stood, causing him to take his hands from me and scoot back. "I'm fine." I stepped around him and put some distance between us. "We should ..." I looked down at the gauze on my shoulder. He hadn't finished closing the scratch. "We should get going."

Slowly, Micah stood and a deep knot appeared between his brows. "Why are you doing this?"

I pulled at the ripped fabric around the scratch, but no matter what, my armor was ruined. "Doing what?"

"Pretending nothing happened."

"But nothing happened."

He crossed his arms and stared at me. "And now you're acting like a teenager."

"What?" I stared at him, appalled. "I am not!" He tilted his head and raised an eyebrow at me. "We don't have time to argue, okay? Let's just get going." I turned my back to him, intent on marching away from the park, but I remembered I didn't know the direction we should go. "Please, can you tell me which way we're going?"

He sighed and soon walked past me. "This way," he said,

taking the lead. I let him walk a few steps in front of me. It was easier than standing side by side with him where it felt too awkward not to talk. But it seemed he didn't want *not* to talk. "Why are you avoiding me?"

Rage, sadness, disappointment, frustration. All of those feelings mixed and made for a heavy ball lodged in my chest. I could continue pretending nothing happened and act like a child, or I could be honest and hope he understood and left me alone after that.

I sighed. "Why do you care if I'm avoiding you? You're the one who always leaves me every time we kissed. You're only upset because this time I was the one who put some distance between us."

"That's—" He shut his mouth, as if considering, as if remembering. He knew I was right. "Believe me, darling, I never *wanted* to leave you."

I scoffed. "Great way of showing it."

Micah halted and stepped in my way. I almost bumped into him.

He towered over me, his stare intense, decisive. "I have never been more honest in my entire long life. I never wanted to leave you. Still don't."

I gulped. "Then why did you leave?"

He ran a hand through his hair and stepped back. "Because of matters out of my control."

"You do realize that's not a great answer."

"It's what I can tell you right now."

Right now? So, he would someday tell me why he always left? When would that be? When I died during the Soul Oath?

"What's your excuse?" he snapped.

"I ... I just don't understand you. We've been on this push

and pull for quite some time now, and I have the feeling you really don't want to be near me. But I keep asking myself, why do you always kiss me? It doesn't make any sense. You confuse me. You make me confused. I never know what to expect from you. And then you up and leave and—"

"For greater reasons I can't tell you about, but I promise you, it was for a good reason."

Why couldn't he tell me? All I could think about was that the gods and goddesses had a hidden agenda, something they weren't telling the rest of us. I felt even more useless than before, if that were possible.

"Even so, it's ridiculous to have hope." Because I would die. Tomorrow or in a week, I would die. There was no point in trying to find out if he really liked me or not.

"Hope of what?"

I shook my head. "Okay, that's enough. We're wasting time talking about something that will never happen." Looking ahead into the darkness of our path, I walked around him. "Let's keep moving."

31

MICAH

Nadine was infuriating and impossibly irresistible.

As we marched across ruins of once famous tourist attractions, I considered stopping her again and either kissing her senseless until she was sure of my feelings for her, or arguing with her. I wanted to demand she tell me what was going on, why she didn't want to tell me the reason she didn't want to have hope. And what she meant by that? Hope of winning the war? Hope of living? Hope of being with me?

More importantly, I wanted to tell her why I left her. I wanted to tell her about the Cup of Life and the hopes I had of saving her.

But I couldn't. Since I had not succeeded, there was no reason to.

In the back of my mind, I started wondering if I should kiss her again and not leave her side until ... until she died. Enjoy the little time we had together. Would she want that?

I shook those thoughts out of my mind when I sensed more demons nearby.

"Demons," I whispered, reaching for Nadine. I held her

arm and pulled back, beside the ruins of a destroyed cathedral.

Though it was not necessary, I held her close to me, her side tucked into my body. I leaned over her and inhaled the scent of her, of her hair, of her skin. By the Everlast, how could I let her die? The simple thought put a huge hole in my chest, one that hurt more and more with every heartbeat.

"I think they are gone," she said, stepping away from me.

She was right, they were retreating, but I was so entranced by her, I hadn't noticed.

I cleared my throat. "Almost gone," I lied.

We waited a couple more minutes before resuming our march toward the Coliseum.

Finally, after walking through Rome for more than seven hours, we spotted the Coliseum in the distance. Before it had only one side collapsed, but now it was all in ruins. Big blocks of limestone and concrete crumbled into a pile of debris.

"I had always dreamed of seeing the world," Nadine said, her voice eerie, low. "I wanted to have the old world back, when it was possible to travel and see these kinds of places." She sighed, and then whispered, "Now I never will."

She hurried her steps before I could react. But what was there to say? "Oh, yeah, even if we win the war, the world won't magically restore itself and be like it was. Besides, you'll be dead and won't see anything."

It made me sick just thinking about it.

We had to hide from another demon battalion on the outskirts of the Coliseum ruins. Once they were out of my aura range, we ran as fast as we could through broken concrete, metal, and stones.

Once we reached the ruins of the Coliseum, Nadine halted.

"What is it?" I asked.

She turned to me, her eyes wide. "I feel ... something."

"Like what?"

"I don't know exactly, and I can't pinpoint it."

"Close your eyes and focus on the feeling."

Nadine shut her eyes, rolled her shoulders and neck, shook her arms loose, and took a long breath. And I waited, anxious.

"It's ... pulsating," she said after a long moment.

"What is pulsating?"

"I don't know." She opened her eyes and stared at me. "A force? An energy?" I tilted my head, thinking. "Don't look at me like I'm crazy. Stuff like this has happened before, and I ended up finding your scepter."

"I'm not looking at you like anything. I'm just thinking."

"About?"

"How incredibly strong and amazing you are."

She rolled her eyes and turned her back to me. "It's coming from there." She pointed to our right, which I thought was the outer ring of the Coliseum.

"Let's follow this force, then, but be careful."

She nodded and set in motion. Getting through the debris wasn't easy. In several points, we had to stop, turn back, and go around it, because going under or through or over was impossible. And going around only increased the time of our mission.

Then, Nadine stopped and pointed to a big block of concrete. "It's under here."

"Under?"

"Yes. I think it's underground."

I groaned. "Of course it is."

She leaned over the block and tried to find a good grip on it. "Help me."

I did help to humor her because I was sure we couldn't raise it, not even with my increased strength.

"I have an idea," I said with a wicked grin. Nadine looked at me with one raised eyebrow, and I almost laughed. She was looking at me like I always looked at her. "Just … stand back. Behind me and farther away, if you can."

"Oh-kay," she said, walking a few yards back.

This wasn't the best idea, but it was the only one I had. I extended my hand in front of me and conjured a black bolt. I analyzed the size and power in it, wondering if I should make it bigger or smaller. Once I thought the size was good for its job, I threw it at the block standing in our way. A boom echoed through the ruins and millions of tiny rock shards flew in all directions. I raised my arms to protect my face, and even so I was pelleted. I felt the tiny rocks hitting me from my chest to my shin.

"Are you crazy?" Nadine asked. I whipped around and stared at her. "That was loud! The demons will come rushing this way."

"I know. An incentive for us to do this shit quickly." I winked.

She gaped at me, as if she still couldn't believe what I had done.

Then, the rubble around Nadine started shaking. The upper half of the wall behind her slid down. Her expression changed from incredulity to pure shock.

"Run!" I cried, reaching for her.

She jumped and grabbed my outstretched hand. I pulled her toward me, and ran to the block I had blasted. But there was nowhere to go. The block was gone, but there was still a stone floor under it. Just a portion of it had broken off in the explosion. I pushed her as far as she could go and covered her with my body as the walls fell around us.

After what seemed like eternity, the trembling stopped and I realized we were still alive. I dared to open my eyes and sucked in a sharp breath. Almost in total darkness, we were under another broken wall, and if it weren't for that, we would have been crushed by the falling rubble.

I pulled away from Nadine enough to produce a bolt in my hand, one that scared off the shadows hiding her beautiful face. She stared at me with big eyes.

"Are you okay?" My eyes roamed, searching her face and what I could see of her body.

"I-I think so."

I let out a long relieved breath. "That was fucking stupid."

"Yeah, it was." Nadine disentangled herself from me, but in this tight space, there was nowhere to go.

"Now what?" I asked. "I thought you said the feeling was coming from under that boulder. The boulder is gone, but there's no passage or doorway under it."

She looked at the floor around us. "There has to be a way." She reached over and swept her hand over the floor, as if it was too dusty and she needed to clean it to see it better.

At her touch, a symbol shone, just a few inches from her fingers.

She gasped. "That's Diana's symbol." She rested her entire hand over it and it shone brighter. The ground began shaking.

"Not again," I hissed, already pulling Nadine to hide under me.

"No, look," she said.

The center of the symbol opened up, and a hole three feet

wide appeared beside Nadine. I raised my hand over it, and the orb illuminated the hole, revealing a long staircase leading down.

"Come on." I helped Nadine shift her weight, so she could go down first, and I followed.

The stairs went down and down and down. The bolt in my hand didn't illuminate much.

"I wasn't claustrophobic," Nadine said. "But I might be now."

If my insides weren't wound tight with anticipation, I would have laughed.

In silence, Nadine and I walked through long, dark, narrow corridors for what seemed like hours.

Finally, we crossed an archway and into what seemed like a big room, since we couldn't see the ends with the light coming from the orb in my hand.

"Here," Nadine said, going farther into the room.

She stopped in front of a pillar four feet high. Diana's symbol was carved on top. Again, Nadine rested her hand over the symbol and it came to life, shining with a white light. Then, we noticed a new light on our left. One crystal sconce on the wall came to life. The one on its left lit up. Then the next one, and the next one, and the next, until all the sconces in the large, round room were shining.

"What is this place?" Nadine whispered.

I had no idea.

In between each sconce, the wall opened to an archway— nine to be exact—but all we could see beyond them was darkness.

"What now?"

"I'm not sure." Her wide eyes jumped from one archway

to the next. "I'm sensing, feeling so many things. All of them pulling at me."

"Is there one that is stronger than the others?"

Nadine closed her eyes and took a deep breath. Slowly, she spun in place, as if testing each one of the archways.

Then she stopped and opened her eyes. She stared dead ahead. "Through this one."

I shrugged. "Then that's where we need to go."

"How can you be so sure?"

"I ... what do you mean?"

"What if this is a test? I mean, Diana was the goddess of justice and courage and wisdom and honesty. It wouldn't be this easy. Just follow the strongest energy. It doesn't make sense." She continued walking, watching the remaining doorways as if they would simply tell her which one housed the spear. "When we went searching for your scepter, I could feel both your scepters. Yours and Victor's. Two equal forces. Nothing more. Why does this place have so many forces calling to me?"

She was thinking out loud and, as much as I wanted to help her, I was lost on this one. I didn't remember Diana, and I had no idea how her mind or her powers worked.

Nadine being Nadine, she did something that totally surprised me. She turned to the short pillar in the center of the room, drew one of the daggers strapped to her boots, and slashed her open palm.

"What—?" I cried.

"Shh," she urged.

Blood pooled in her hand and she let a few drops fall on the symbol carved on top of the pillar. Instantly, the symbol's shine grew brighter and several lines sprouted from it. The straight lines went down the edge and sides of the pillar, reaching the floor, and traveled toward the doors along the walls. But all the lines stopped halfway through the room, except for one. One of the lines went until it disappeared through the archway.

"That way," she said with a small smile. She pulled gauze and tape from her backpack. I took both from her.

I stared at her, amazed. "How did you know?" I lowered my gaze to her hand and focused on cleaning and covering the shallow cut on her palm.

"I saw something similar in my dreams. I don't know why I decided to try it now, but well, I'm glad it worked." She cleaned her dagger with another piece of gauze, and then stashed it back in the side of her boot. "Let's go."

We followed the bright white line on the ground and went through the archway into what looked like a maze— several corners and turns and doorways. Every couple dozen feet, a few steps took us down more, and we went deeper and deeper into the earth. Finally, the bright line followed a long path until it bumped into a wall and went up to the middle of the wall.

Nadine didn't hesitate. She rested her palm at the end of the line and the symbol appeared again. The wall trembled and dissolved, much like the ground had done before, revealing a room past it.

Right in the middle of the small square chamber, the spear floated in a cloud of bright white light.

"Wow," Nadine whispered, echoing my thoughts. The spear was beautiful with a crystal body and a sharp end. She took a step toward it and I closed my hand around her wrist, holding her back.

"What if it's booby trapped?"

She glanced at me as if I were crazy. "Why would it be?

Nothing we took so far was booby trapped." She was right, as usual.

I released her. "Just be careful."

A small smile adorned her lips, betraying the harsh shake of her head. "I will be."

She went to the spear, reached for it, and wrapped her fingers along the shaft.

The bright light disappeared, only to appear again in the blade of the spear. The bright light traveled through the shaft until it touched Nadine's hand. It then traveled into Nadine's skin, a white line that went up her arm and shoulder to her chest. She raised her eyes to me. I wanted to reach to her, I wanted to help her, but we had seen similar actions before, and it had all been part of the ritual, of what was supposed to happen. I didn't want to touch her, to help her, and risk interfering.

The line reached her heart. It disappeared for a second, only to explode the next moment, a bright light that blinded me. I shielded my eyes as Nadine gasped.

Soon enough the light was gone and Nadine was on her knees, grasping the spear with both hands.

Now her aura felt more like Alice's, but a little different. Stronger. Like the high-ranked lady of Diana that she was.

"Are you okay?" I asked, reaching for her. I closed my hand around her elbow and helped her up.

She stared at the spear. "I-I think so."

"Feeling different?"

"A little," she muttered.

My attention snapped as I felt hundreds of demons closing in on us. "When you touched the spear ... the demons must have felt something because they are coming this way.

Apparently, the magic also broke the barrier around Rome." I held her hand firmer in mine. "Ready?"

Still with a dazed gleam in her eyes, Nadine nodded.

I teleported us out of there.

Nadine looked around, her eyes narrowing. "Where are we?"

32

NADINE

"My little place in the underworld," Micah said.

I looked around, taking in the space. A big room with shiny, black flooring, dark red walls, a thick rug, velvet chaise lounges, a complete bar to the side, and a huge crystal chandelier hanging from the ceiling.

"Why did you bring me here?"

"Because I couldn't think. I just teleported us out of there." He dropped my hand but stayed close, his eyes on me. "Are you okay?" he asked me again.

His question brought more pressing matters to the front of my mind.

"I guess so." I was okay but different. I could now feel the magic in me. Diana's magic. I looked at my left hand. It still looked the same. The right one did too, though it was wrapped around the Spear of Justice.

It was too much—the sudden memories filling my mind, the feelings bursting in my chest. Even though I was only a lady of Diana, it was as if I knew everything about her.

Micah clutched my upper arms. "I know it's too much.

Believe me, I know." He ran his hands up and down my arms. "If someone can get through this, if someone can make sense of all of it and keep moving, it's you."

I forced a smile, but the corner of my lips barely moved. "Thanks."

Micah stepped back. "Do you want something to drink?"

I shook my head, and then noticed my throat was parched and nodded. "Water, please."

In front of the bar along the wall, Micah let out a loud laugh. "Water. That's one thing I don't think I have here." I wouldn't be surprised if he was serious—I recognized scotch, vodka, tequila, martini, champagne, and wine bottles. But no water. He then turned to his backpack and took one water bottle from there. "Here you go." He handed the bottle to me.

"Thanks." I sat down on a velvet chaise lounge and drank half the bottle in three big gulps.

Then I set the bottle aside and rested the spear along my lap. It was beautiful with a crystal body and a white blade at one of the ends. It looked seriously sharp. And it thrummed with power. Each time I touched it, I felt it. Strong, unyielding, just, courageous, wise.

Just like Diana. Just like me.

"This is crazy," I whispered, still having a hard time wrapping my head around this new development. I mean, not that I doubted it when Victor had first mentioned it, but thinking about it, imagining it, was different from actually living it.

Micah sat on the other chaise lounge. "I know." He pointed to my shoulder. "You should be able to heal other people now. Why don't you give it a try?"

The scratch was still ugly looking, but, with all the agitation of the past couple of days, I barely felt it. Still, it would be better if it was healed and not prone to any infection.

I sucked in a sharp breath. "All right." I did the same thing I had always done with Micah and Victor. With my hand resting over the wound, I closed my eyes and imagined my power, my energy traveling from my core to the wound, cleaning it, gluing it, closing it. Warmth surged from around the scratch. I opened my eyes and gasped when I saw the cut healing. After a few seconds, it was all done. The skin was smooth and fair again. No sign of any injury. "That's ... incredible."

One corner of Micah's lips tugged up. "It really is."

I lowered my hand as a sudden feeling invaded my chest, making it hard to breathe. I was sad for having to leave. "Maybe it's time to go."

As soon as the words left my mouth, I knew I didn't want to leave. Not yet. Because once Micah dropped me outside the wards in NYC, that was it. Our army would be gathered and tomorrow we would march on Imha. I would probably only see Micah again during the fight, and after we hopefully won, my time would be up. He and I would conclude the Soul Oath.

And I would never have told him how I felt.

Boldness exploded in my chest, and I choked on the words that were rushing through my mouth.

Gripping the spear hard, I stood and faced him. "This might be the last time we're alone and not in a run-for-your-life situation, so I need to tell you something." His brow pinched and I almost lost the courage to continue. Almost. I sucked in a deep breath and pushed through anyway. "Before I die, I need to tell you that I love you." I swallowed, shocked I had actually said it. His eyes widened in surprise. "I first realized I loved you when you brought me to the underworld to see my family, but I think I started loving you much—" With his eyes hard and his lips pressed tight, Micah rose and I stepped back. "—sooner than that." He advanced toward me, and by the look on his face, I was sure he was going to hit me. Or shake me. Or teleport me to NYC before I could embarrass myself further. "Anyway, I just thought you should know." I extended my hand between us. "Now you can take me back to the others."

Micah closed his hand around mine and he pulled me hard to him. I almost lost my hold on the spear. Now, up close, I could clearly see I had misinterpreted the hard look in his eyes. He wasn't angry or disgusted. He was hungry. For me.

I gasped as one of his hand wound around my waist and the other caught the spear from me and placed it on one of the chaise lounges. Then his hand was around my neck and his face leaned down, his mouth only one inch from mine.

"I love you too, darling," he whispered. "I love you too damn much."

Before I could process his confession, his lips crashed on mine and erased everything else from my mind. There was only us.

At that moment, I surrendered myself to him, body and soul. I had always been his; he had owned me even before the Soul Oath. His kiss was ardent, starving, deep, and I matched each move and each stroke. I tangled my arms around his neck, molding my body to his, wanting to touch him, to feel every inch of him.

His tongue teased mine and I moaned. At that, he pulled back and groaned. Taking advantage of the separation, I tugged his shirt up. He lifted an eyebrow at me, a question in his eyes.

Warmth seeped in my cheeks, and I said, "I love you, Micah, and I want you to make love to me."

His eyes widened for a second and he groaned again. Without another moment of hesitation, Micah pulled his shirt over his head and threw it aside. And I let my eyes fleet over his gorgeous, rippled chest and abdomen. However, his new tattoo caught my attention.

I grazed my fingertips on what looked like the center of the tattoo, right above his heart. "How ... how is it longer?"

He rested his hand over mine and pressed my palm against his heart. His heartbeat was accelerated and the up and down of his chest erratic.

"Because it's not a tattoo," Micah said, his voice somber.

"What is it, then?"

"Is it okay if I explain later? Right now I have more important things to do." His eyes traveled up and down my body. He licked his lips, the shine of hunger becoming brighter in his eyes.

I smiled, loving how he looked at me. "Show me what these important things are," I whispered.

Micah hissed. Then he hooked his arms under my shoulders and my knees and walked with me past the chaise lounges. I had no idea where he was taking me until an archway appeared out of nowhere in the wall. He walked past it with me into what looked like a massive, elegant bedroom with a big four-post bed with black gossamer curtains and black silk sheets. With his eyes boring holes into mine, he carried me to the bed and gently deposited me right in the middle.

Micah crawled on top of me. He placed his hands flat on the pillow on each side of my head, his dark gaze searching my face.

"Are you sure?"

I lifted myself on my elbows and grazed my lips on his. "I've never been surer in my entire life." I wound my arms around his neck and my legs around his waist, and pulled him down on me. He groaned, taking my mouth again, and I moaned with how delicious his weight felt on me.

There was only us, and then the two of us became one—our bodies tangled together in the silk sheets, skin on skin, our breaths mingled in a frantic rhythm. My heart was about to explode with the righteousness of it all. It was as if we belonged together, as if there was nothing else in the world but us. I never thought I could feel this way, this love, this passion—about what we were doing and about him.

And deep inside, I kept wishing this moment would never, ever end.

"I SHOULDN'T GO MUCH FARTHER," MICAH SAID, ONE HAND around my waist, keeping me close to him.

It was late morning and we were in the middle of a dying forest. Micah had teleported us four times already since we left the underworld.

After we made love last evening, Micah convinced me to stay with him for the night.

"Levi won't be waiting for you until tomorrow," he had said. "And this will be the only time we have alone."

His argument was compelling, but in the end I stayed because I wanted to.

Later that night, he teleported out and brought us dinner, and while we ate, he told me about his fight against the Death Lords and about the poisonous web spreading through his body. I jumped into action, trying to formulate a plan, a way of saving him, of stopping the poison, of making him whole again. I even tried healing him, but apparently a lady of Diana wasn't *that* strong of a healer. However, he said he wasn't worried about that, not yet. We had more important things to focus on. I knew he was right, but that didn't make me any less worried about him. He robbed me of my thoughts when he kissed me and took me to bed again, where we made love again before falling asleep in each other's arms. It had been the best sleep I had in a long time—nightmare-less and feeling completely safe. In the morning, Micah repeated the process, but in the opposite order. We made love, and then he went out to bring us breakfast. Then it was time to go.

I shook my head, forcing myself back to the present. "Because of your aura?"

Micah nodded. "All of our allies are supposed to be in New York, getting ready for the battle. If I stay there too long, they will sense me. We aren't sure who we can trust, so it's better if they all think I'm still on Imha's side until the last minute."

My stomach dropped. "I understand." Trying to appease the despair taking hold of me, I gripped the hilt of the sword hanging from the belt on my waist. It was the spear disguised as a simple sword. Micah's idea so nobody would stare at me and wonder what the hell I was up to. His way of keeping the spear and its function a secret.

"So I'm just gonna teleport us there, and I'll instantly teleport out."

"Are you saying goodbye now?"

One corner of his lips quirked up. "I'm trying." He slipped

a hand around my neck and cupped my nape. "Gods, I don't want to leave you."

I held on to his shirt as his forehead touched mine. "I don't want to leave you either."

He brushed his lips on mine. "Please, be careful, darling."

"I'll be with Ceris and Victor and Alice. You're the one with the enemy. You should be *really* caref—"

He silenced me with a kiss. A desperate, deep, harsh, long kiss that left my soul raw, my heart in pieces. After a long while, he withdrew his lips but kept his head close to mine.

"I love you," I whispered.

"I love you more," he said.

I was about to protest, but then the world spun and blinked and the next thing I knew I was standing outside the barrier in New York. Alone.

Even knowing he wouldn't be beside me anymore, I looked around, hoping to get one last glimpse of him.

I sighed, checked to see if my uniform was still okay—save for the bloodied, ripped shoulder—if my hair was in place, and if the sword was still secured on my waist. As soon as I crossed the barrier, everyone would be able to sense me, feel how my aura was different, and they all would look at me.

Regardless, I had to go on.

After a long breath, I crossed the barrier and started walking toward the building where our apartment was hidden. Two turns later, I started seeing our allies camped along the path—and they were all standing, looking at me as if I were a one-woman parade. I had to admit, I didn't think we had this many allies—I couldn't count fast enough, but if I had to guess, I would say there were about two thousand deities and supporters gathered around our apartment. And, as I walked by, they all gawked at me as if I were a creature with seven heads.

About fifty yards from the front doors of the building, Ceris and Victor poofed right in front of me. Startled, I skidded to a halt and almost bumped into them.

"Want to give me a heart attack, jeez!" I snapped, trying to calm my racing heart.

They both stared at me with giant eyes.

"Where's the spear?" Ceris asked, her voice low. Staring at her, I touched the sword again, hoping she would get my message. She lowered her gaze to the weapon and her eyes lit up with wonder. What? She had so little faith in me she thought I wouldn't be able to retrieve it?

"Your aura," Victor said. "We can tell you're the same as Alice's, but there's still something off."

Ceris turned her wide eyes to me. "It's like you're more than her."

"More powerful," I added. That was what Micah suggested, though I didn't feel powerful. "Maybe because of my higher rank?"

"By the Everlast," Victor whispered.

"That's ... amazing." Ceris smiled.

"So," I started. "I know you guys want to know all about my quest and I want to know all about what happened here." I glanced around to the curious people gathering. "But can we do it inside?"

"Of course," Victor said.

Ceris touched my arm and poofed us both inside. Victor met us there.

Frowning, I glanced around and realized why they had transported us to their bedroom. "You don't want the others to know about the spear."

Victor nodded. "We know we have a traitor, but we don't know who, so until we find out we want to keep the spear a secret."

"All right." It made sense, though depending on who our traitor was, he or she would be able to sense my new aura. He or she would know something was different. Well, that was a problem to think about later. Exhausted, I sat down in an armchair in the corner of their room. "So, what do you want to know first?"

33

MICAH

THE FIRST TIME I WALKED THROUGH THESE GATES HAD BEEN painful.

This time though, it felt like having a new Black Thorn rip through my chest with each step. I didn't want to be here, I didn't want to see Imha again, I didn't want to stand in front of her and pretend I was on her side.

I took a deep breath and entered Imha's improvised throne room.

"My dear Mitrus," she cooed from her throne. "It's so good to see you."

I approached her. "I see everything is going well here."

"It's wonderful." Her eyes shone with wicked light and her smile widened, becoming even more crazed than before. "I've received your reports. Well done, Mitrus. I knew you still had it in you."

I just nodded because really, what would I say? I didn't have it in me to push myself that far. "What is our next move?"

Imha pouted. Not a pretty sight. "Oh, so serious and direct. You need to learn to have fun again." She strolled to me, moving her hips more than necessary. "I can show you how."

It took everything in me not to flinch. "Maybe another time. After we win the war."

"We're close to winning, dear." She circled me, looking me up and down, as if she were appraising me like a pig, seeing if it was fat enough for the table. She clicked her tongue. "My spy informed me of Levi's next move. They plan on taking over one of my training camps in two days' time. Stupid," she muttered. "We'll be there, waiting for them. We'll end this war once and for all."

"Sounds like a good plan. When are we leaving?"

"I've already sent several of my generals, but we'll go tomorrow. Just to make sure we are there, prepared for the final battle, even before they set foot there." Imha ran her finger across my shoulders. "Which means we have time ..." She didn't finish it, probably expecting me to.

Once more, I fought the urge to jerk away from her, from her touch.

"To rest and get ready," I added, hoping I sounded bored. "After all I did these past few days, I need to rest." Turning to her, I caught her hand in mine and forced a half grin to stamp my lips. My eyes fixed on her, I leaned down and kissed the back of her hand. "I'll see you later."

Later as in right after she left for the battle tomorrow. Until then, I would hide, pretending I was too busy to notice anything else.

Her dark eyes glinted with mischief. "Certainly," she purred.

I winked and walked past her. Once she couldn't see my face, my grin slipped away and my lips turned upside down. A deep shudder took root in the base of my spine, but I held it back until I was out of the throne room and out of sight.

Now, if only I could stay out of *her* sight for the next twenty-four hours.

34

NADINE

WE WERE ALL HERE. VICTOR, CERIS, IZAERA, ZELEN, MAHO, Sol, Ronen, Alice, and me. Except for Micah. Besides Victor and me, no one knew he was actually on our side.

My heart ached a little looking at everyone now, all dressed up in our beige uniforms, with combat boots and heavily armed with weapons, standing together in the living room of our apartment. We were still missing two great allies, and there was no way to get them back. Morgan and Keisha. How I wished they could join us today. Their strength and their energy would be missed.

Maho started pacing. "Are you sure Imha will be at the training camp?" he asked.

"We're hoping she will be," Ceris said. "Either way, if she's not, that's where most of her army is located. We take them down and then we go after her regardless of where she is."

"And how will you find out where she is?" Sol asked.

"We will torture it from one of her generals," Victor said, sounding calm. Then he straightened and cleared his throat.

"Everyone ready?" Some of us uttered "yes" while others just nodded.

Together we climbed down the stairs and exited the building. We stopped in front of the thousands of allies gathered outside. From the looks of it—tactical clothing, heavy boots, and weapons strapped to belts or hooks—everyone was ready for battle.

I thought Victor would stand up on an improvised platform and deliver a few words of encouragement to our army, but all he did was raised his closed fist and yell, "Let's kick Imha's ass!"

A roaring cheer erupted from our allies. Then we all marched until we were on the other side of the protective shield and teleported to the place we were meant to go.

35

MICAH

IMHA AND OMI LEFT WITH NEARLY EIGHTY PERCENT OF THE army she had housed in this castle. I left with them, but then when she was too busy and focused on her tasks, I teleported back.

I called all the demons left in the castle to the throne room and told them to wait for me as I had important information to deliver. Meanwhile, I went to the gates and unlocked them, undoing the magic Imha and Omi had conjured to secure the estate.

In the distance, I saw a red spot against the dark top of a hill. The signal that they were here.

A feeling of unease settled in my stomach as I walked back into the villa's main building. I wasn't nervous or thinking this over—I just wanted to get this done so we could move on.

In the throne room, the demons grew restless. They looked side to side, growled at each other, as if I didn't give some important order soon, they would become too bored and start ripping each other's throats out.

Which was all right by me.

A few tense minutes passed.

We're here, Victor said in my mind. *In position.*

About time, I answered.

"All right, all right," I said out loud. The demons quieted down and turned to me. "I have some important news to deliver to you."

On cue my allies dropped the veil over their auras and burst through the doors and windows of the throne room—Nadine, Levi, Ceris, Izaera, Zelen, Alice, Ronen, Maho, Sol, and many other deities. They fell on the demons and didn't give them a chance to fight back.

With pure rage in her eyes, Ceris came at me, but Levi stepped in her way. "He's on our side," he said out loud, so everyone could hear him.

Her jaw fell open and her eyes widened. "W-what?"

Behind them, everyone else, but Nadine, faltered. They engaged the demons, but their attention was on us.

"I'll explain later," Levi said. "Now we have a fight to win." He turned to the demons and, after staring at me for another few seconds, Ceris shook off her shock and commenced fighting the demons.

I fought too, but most of my attention was on Nadine, looking super-hot in her repaired uniform and a sword in her hand. She cut through the demons like water until she was fighting by my side.

I couldn't help but smile. "Hi, darling," I said, throwing a black bolt at the chest of a demon. The bolt exploded on its chest. The demon crumbled into ashes soon after.

"Hi," Nadine said, sounding a little timid. She knelt to avoid a claw and brought her sword up, slashing the demon's gut. It fell on the floor, in a pool of gooey blood, and she stood up, smiling at me.

By the Everlast, I wanted to sweep her in my arms and kiss her senseless.

But a demon lunged at me and I had to kiss it instead.

Not even ten minutes after it started, this battle was over.

Nadine turned to me and I turned to her, both of us already reaching for the other. In two seconds, my arms were around her waist and my mouth on hers.

"Gods, I missed you," I said, before sealing my lips on hers again and kissing her like she deserved it. Nadine's body melted into mine. Gods, I loved the feel of her, the scent of her, the taste of her. I loved all of her.

Someone cleared his or her throat. Nadine and I broke apart—though my arm was still around her waist and nobody would be able to get it off there—to see the rest of gang approaching us.

"That was easy," Levi said, serious.

"So," Ceris started, sounding wary, "you were on our side the entire time?"

"Yup," I said.

Maho looked from Levi to me. "Why all this mystery? Why tell us we were going to Imha's training camp instead of here, and why not tell us about Mitrus working for us?"

"Yeah," Sol said, a deep frown between his brows. "I do not take being lied to lightly."

"That was quite a surprise," Ronen said, sounding amused.

Levi stood tall. "Mitrus was working *with us*," Levi corrected Maho before glancing at me, a meaning hidden under his brief stare. "Let's just say it was necessary."

The uneasiness hung around our group and I thought it wouldn't wear off easily.

I scanned around. The throne room looked like a slaughterhouse. Our side didn't have any deaths, but I could see a few deities bleeding—nothing worrying. Most of the demons were dead, and about two dozen were gathered in the center of the room, being watched by Ceris and other deities and held by magic.

Ceris nodded toward us and we nodded back. Then she teleported out, taking the demons with her. The plan was to take survivors to the island in Croatia, where Ceris had worked her magic and said no one, no demon, no deity could get out without her to undo her spell.

While Ceris was out, Nadine walked around the room, using her new and improved healing abilities on the deities with the worst wounds.

Ten minutes later, Ceris was back with us. "We should keep moving," she said.

"Where's the portal?" Levi asked me.

"Through here." I took Nadine's hand in mine and led them to the back of the castle, where a curved shallow pool complemented the garden.

When we approached the pool, our symbols appeared as bright lights in the water's surface. One by one, we walked into the pool, using our powers to walk on the surface, and stepped on our symbols.

Levi, Ceris, Izaera, Maho, Ronen, Sol, and I extended our hands in front of us and our scepters appeared in our hands. We bumped the scepters three times on strategic places of our symbols, and a new light appeared in the center of our symbols, forming a big, united circle. Bright light shone through it until it reached the skies.

The portal was open.

They all stepped into the light. I turned to Nadine and beckoned her to come with me. Looking a little wary, she walked to me, caught my hand, and we marched through the portal together.

36

NADINE

I had seen the Clarity Castle in my visions and in my dreams, but I had never thought I would actually see it with my eyes.

We emerged from the reflective pool in the throne room. The crystal thrones around the crystal pool—all as I remembered, but it all was also new to me. I gawked at the place as the rest of our army came in through the pool.

Ceris and Victor took charge and assigned posts and places for everyone that came through the portal—almost three thousand people. We had more allies, almost another thousand according to Ceris, but she had sent them to the training camp to distract Imha while we took over the Clarity Castle.

Their orders were to distract, not to engage. We didn't want to put their lives at risk. If Imha engaged before she heard of our takeover, then they were supposed to flee until we were able to regroup. The bigger our army, the stronger we were.

Still holding my hand, Micah guided me to one of the

archways behind the throne room. From there, he took me to a grand staircase made of crystal, and to the next floor, which had a balcony overlooking the back of the throne room.

"You'll hide here," Micah said. "Once Imha emerges through the pool, you throw the spear at her."

I nodded, feeling a little nervous thread taking root in my chest. I rolled my shoulders. "I can do this," I whispered.

Micah cupped my face with his hands and stared into my eyes. I was lost in the dark abyss of his gaze. "You *can* do this."

I sighed. A girl-in-love kind of sigh.

Taking advantage of every second we had together, I stood on my tiptoes and brushed my lips against his. Micah groaned before kissing me for real. My lips parted and his tongue teased mine. I loved him and I loved kissing him—his lips on mine had become one of my favorite things.

"You two do realize we're getting ready for the biggest battle yet, right?"

Micah sighed against my lips before throwing a black bolt at Ceris's feet. "Go away."

"Hey!" She jumped back. I put my hand over my mouth to hide the laugh bubbling in my throat. "This is not a joke," she chided.

"Sorry, Ceris," I said after I was sure I could talk without breaking into a fit of giggles. "Micah was about to go to his spot."

She humphed and left.

After we found Victor's and Micah's scepters, I thought Ceris and I had broken an invisible wall that had prevented us from being friends before. We were never Cheryl and Nadine again, but we were slowly discovering a new kind of friendship. Until I became a lady of Diana, and Micah and I became what looked like a couple. She now seemed to hate my guts again.

"She's just jealous," Micah said as we watched Ceris walk away, stopping every two seconds to make sure everyone was in the right position, with the right weapon, in the right state of mind.

"Of you and me?"

"Not of you and me but of what we have." He glanced down from the balcony to where Victor stood, talking to some deities. "Levi and she still aren't the same as before, and I think she knows it'll never be the same again."

And what did we have? Here we were, pretending to have a "normal" relationship when he was immortal and I had a death sentence. Soon I would be dead and there would be no relationship.

"Hey." Micah brushed his fingertips along my cheek. "What's with that pouty face?"

I shook it off and smiled at him. "Nothing." I planted a quick kiss on his lips. "You should go."

"I will, darling, but only after a proper kiss."

Clasping a hand around my nape and with his arm secured around my waist, Micah dipped me backward and kissed me. His lips were soft against mine, but the kiss wasn't. It was harsh, desperate, as if this was the last time we would kiss and he wanted to make it count. To have it engraved into his mind, into his soul.

Then he broke the kiss, let go of me, and walked away as if he couldn't bear to say goodbye.

"Good luck," I whispered to his retreating back.

When he disappeared behind a doorway, I looked over the balcony. Everyone was moving about, checking his or her weapons, traps, and tricks.

A trickle of fear ran through me, icing my veins. I let out a shaky breath.

Only a handful knew about the spear and my role in this battle, but in the end, they were all counting on me. If I could hit Imha as soon as she appeared through the portal, there would be no fight. Nobody here had to risk his or her lives. The war would be over. Only if I got it right.

What if I didn't get it right? What if I missed? Imha and her army would come charging into the Clarity Castle and a real battle would begin. And it wouldn't be as quick as when we invaded the throne room in her castle in England. This time, we would have thousands of people and she would have thousands of demons. It would be a bloody mess. And—

I closed my eyes and shut those thoughts out.

Now was not the time to let doubt creep in. Now was not the time to imagine everything that could go wrong. The only thing I had to focus on was making that shot.

"I can do this," I whispered to myself.

Then, a scout came through the portal. "They are here!" he shouted.

A second of silence. The next second, everyone was hustling about, the ones that weren't in the right position ran and yelled.

"Quickly!" Ceris said, her voice booming across the throne room. She, Victor, Micah, Izaera, Maho, Ronen, and Sol were positioned between their thrones and the reflective pool in a wide arc. As the strongest, they insisted on being the front line, to eliminate any weak threat quickly, as Micah had put it.

Alice and the lesser gods and goddesses stood behind them—our second strongest group. Hopefully, the battle would be quick and the deaths would be minimal.

Fifteen seconds later, it was as if a blanket had fallen over us, muting every one of our sounds, even our erratic breathing and thumping hearts.

I reached down to my belt and pulled the spear-in-the-form-of-a-sword from its scabbard. The power of the spear thrummed against my hands, and I wondered if anyone could guess that I wasn't really holding a sword. I glanced down at the weapon. It was still hard to swallow how I could touch it, how I could use it. Could I use it? Would it work? What if, in my hands, it didn't work as it was supposed to?

Focus, Nadine!

I put one leg in front of the other, in a fighting stance, and grabbed the sword by its hilt. With one simple thought, it would change from sword to spear. I just had to wait for the right moment.

A dozen demons came through the portal first, quickly followed by another dozen, and then another dozen. The gods and goddesses were able to take care of most of them quickly, but a large number escaped between them. The demons were met with the meat of our army, but because of the limited space in the throne room, we weren't thinning them out quickly.

On the balcony on the other side of the room, archers waited for an opportunity to fire, which wasn't easy considering how close everyone stood.

I groaned, wishing I could do more than stand here and watch the pool. I wanted to fight too! I wanted to keep an eye on Micah, make sure he was okay.

Another trickle of fear sliced through me, telling me that Imha could emerge in the middle of the demons, hidden behind them, and I could miss her.

More demons came. And more. And more.

And nothing of Imha and Omi.

Surging from the stairwell, demons made their way to me. In a flash, Micah was at my side, killing them as quickly as they came, then he teleported back to the front line.

In that moment, my focus had shifted. I had glanced at the demons coming, then at Micah. What if Imha had sneaked in then?

I cursed, calling myself all the names I knew and some that I invented. Stupid, stupid, stupid.

But it was impossible not to look around. Bodies and blood covered the floors, and in the mess it was hard to identify which side had more bodies down.

Purple smoke exploded from the reflective pool, shaking the ground and the walls. I fell on my knees. Micah and the others flew back several feet.

The smoke dissipated, revealing about ten lesser gods and goddesses surrounding Imha and Omi, who stood right in the middle of the pool, looking regal and powerful.

Quickly, I got to my feet, transformed the sword into a spear, aimed, and threw. Directly at her chest.

Imha looked surprised as she twisted her body and let the spear fly past.

"Ouch, Nadine." She offered me a big, sarcastic smile. "I thought we were friends."

I gaped in disbelief.

I missed.

I missed.

Oh my God, I had missed.

"And you, Mitrus." Imha tsked, her eyes on him. "I'm so disappointed."

Ceris recovered from the blast and stepped forward. "The Clarity Castle is ours. Surrender now, Imha!"

Imha let out a loud, evil laugh. "Never!"

Then Sol lunged at Ceris, but she ducked and he took Izaera instead. Her back to his chest, Sol wrapped his arm around Izaera's neck and held a Black Thorn to her chest.

"What the ...?" Maho muttered, his voice breaking.

Sol retreated two steps, getting closer to Imha. "Stand back!" he yelled. "Stand back or I'll kill her!"

The gods and goddesses took a couple of steps back but didn't lower their guard. The throne room thrummed with tension and anticipation.

"Oh, didn't you know?" Imha said, her tone amused. "Sol here was working for me the entire time." She snapped her fingers and Lua—a hurt, dirty, shackled Lua—appeared at her feet.

So ... so ... Imha had Lua all this time? That was why I could never find her?

"I did my part," Sol grunted, his eyes on our group.

Imha sighed, sounding bored. "A deal is a deal." She snapped her fingers again, and the shackles around Lua's ankles and wrists disappeared.

Sol pushed Izaera toward Omi, who grabbed her with much more efficiency, and rushed to Lua. She jerked away from him, as if disgusted by what he had done. For her.

"Lua, please," Sol muttered.

Bored, Imha stepped around them. A smile crept over her face as she raised her hands above her head. "Kill them!"

Armed with Black Thorns and swords, the lesser gods and goddesses on Imha's side advanced.

Imha and Omi stayed by the pool while the battle commenced. Our gods engaged the lesser gods, while the demons advanced, taking on our deities. And Sol caught Lua in his arms and retreated to the back of the throne room.

I couldn't just sit here and wait for the spear to appear by my side. I had to go find it, and on my way, I could help with the fighting.

I drew my real sword from its scabbard and turned around, thinking of taking the stairs. But before I could reach them, a swarm of demons came up and faced me. I didn't hesitate. I raised my sword and lunged at them.

37

MICAH

Imha had targeted me. I guess she didn't like being betrayed.

She threw a purple bolt at me, one after the one, and I rolled out of the way. My back hit the first step around the pool, and I braced my hands on it to help me stand.

Imha didn't give up. She screeched as she flung a big, purple bolt at me. I jumped to my feet, avoiding it completely. The bolt hit the pool. A loud boom resonated across the throne room. The pool broke in half, and water spilled on the floor around it.

"What ...?" Levi inhaled sharply.

The crack in the middle of the crystal pool began opening up, more and more, until it was a huge hole in the floor. And a huge, crystal-like creature stepped out of it. I gawked, taking in the translucent creature that had bones and muscles and veins intertwined with crystals. Its arms and legs were long and thick and its head was massive, with a big mouth and sharp teeth. The monster opened its arms, showing off the long crystals claws at the end of its hands. After scanning the area once, the monster let out a huge roar. The ground and walls shook again.

"What is that?" Alice asked, somewhere behind me.

"I don't know," Nadine whispered.

I did a double take, not expecting to see Nadine standing here. I thought she was still on the balcony, waiting for her next opportunity to hit Imha with the spear.

"It's the Lucent," Maho explained to them. "He's the Clarity Castle's protector."

That was a nice way to put it.

"So he's going to help us?" Nadine said, sounding relieved.

Maho scoffed. "He attacks whoever is putting the castle at risk, and right now we're all destroying the castle."

Lucent roared again and swiped one big claw around the fountain. Several deities had to jump back, but some were still hit. He fished for the deities and demons, closing both hands around two and then three of them. He threw the three in his right hand at the wall across the room. The deities hit the wall with a loud thud, and then fell to the floor, from where they didn't get up. Then, Lucent lifted his hand with the other two above his head. He tilted his head back, opening his mouth wide.

"Oh my God," Nadine gasped as he ate them.

"Maho! Izaera! Ronen!" Ceris yelled. "On Lucent! Now!"

The gods and goddesses came forward and engaged the big monster. They taunted him, trying to make him leave, but he never went more than ten yards from the pool.

As if a switch had been flipped, the fighting commenced, and Imha threw another bolt at me.

I conjured a shield wall and turned to Nadine, glancing at her hands. "Darling, where's the spear?"

"I lost it when I first threw it at Imha," she said.

I cursed and scanned the area. I couldn't see the damn spear. "I'll keep Imha entertained. Go find the spear." She nodded. A new bolt hit the shield and I put more power into it, making it stronger. "Use your senses!" I yelled as Nadine ducked under the claws of a demon and disappeared among the sea of enemies.

"Stop hiding behind your shield, coward!" Imha taunted me.

I tossed a bolt at her and moved, drawing her away from where Nadine was headed. When Imha flung another bolt at me, I put the shield back up. Breathing hard, I took account of our forces. Zelen had fallen and Izaera seemed to be overwhelmed, fighting too many at the same time. Sol was fighting Imha's demons *and* our allies, while trying to protect a weakened Lua. Ronen and Maho were in charge of Lucent, but it was getting harder and harder to trick the big creature. Ceris had been grazed by a Black Thorn on her arm and was struggling to keep fighting. She had fallen back and was now fighting demons. Levi had Omi for himself, while I had Imha. It was all too balanced, too perfectly matched. Unless we came up with an advantage soon, we would keep fighting for days, until our strength drained and we simply gave up.

When we thought Imha was done bringing more shit into the Clarity Castle, mist rose from the broken pool and more demons appeared. Then a dozen more. Then another dozen.

Imha cackled like a mad witch. "Surround them!" she yelled.

Swiftly, the new arrivals formed a circle around Levi and me and started taunting us, attacking us, trying to break our focus, to make us cave.

Omi stepped away from the circle. "I think you got things

covered here, my dear," he said to Imha. His gaze went past her, past the sea of demons around us. "I have an old toy to play with."

What?

Panic rose in my chest as I watched him disappear in the crowd, headed to where Nadine had gone.

"No!" I yelled, trying to go after him. However, Imha and more demons were in my way, and all I could do was hope.

38

NADINE

Fighting demons, I advanced toward the place where I thought the spear had fallen.

"How can I help?" Alice asked over the grunts, the clang of metal, and the screams.

I almost told her I had this, but then I considered it for a second. This was it. I had to find this damn spear and use it on Imha. There was no other plan to win this war. And if she could help me do it, great—even if it meant deviating from her first assignment of securing the second line of defense with the lesser gods and goddesses. Finding the spear and having one of us hold it and use it was key.

"Just ... watch my back," I said, trying to focus on two things at once: the attacks from demons and the floor, where I thought the spear would be, forgotten like a fallen sword from a dead soldier.

She grunted in response, already engaging a demon that had lunged for me.

I struck a demon that had been in my way and pushed its

heavy body aside. Behind it, I saw another demon, picking the spear up from the floor.

Relief and panic seized my chest. I had found it! But it was in the wrong hands!

But that panic was nothing compared to what I felt when Omi stepped in front of the demon and grabbed the spear from it. My heart and my breathing stopped.

With a haunting grin, Omi turned to me. "Looking for this?" He weighed the spear in his hand. "I saw you throw this at Imha. What is it?"

I gulped, not failing to notice that the demons had stepped away, giving Omi and me more space. It was as if he had said, "She's mine!" and they all retreated. I didn't let that scare me. Instead, I let my mind churn with ideas of how to take the spear from the man who had murdered my family. Oh, how I wished I was a fan of torture because Omi deserved it.

Behind me, Alice stiffened, but she didn't stop fighting the demons that got too close.

Omi twisted the spear in his hands. "It must be important; otherwise you wouldn't have that shocked expression on your pretty face." He started walking around the circle, his gait that of a drunk man, and his gaze shifting between the spear and me. "Is it shock? Perhaps it's fear. Fear of me. Fear of what I did, of what I can do." His sneer widened and the glint of his brown eyes shone almost as crazy as Imha's. "Tell me, my dear Nadine, are you afraid I will do to you what I did to your parents? Are you going to beg like those puny, little humans did?"

That did it.

I snarled and lunged at him.

But I didn't get far. He threw a bolt at me, and I had to sidestep it. Then Omi started sending bolt after bolt, and I didn't stop moving—rolling, ducking, jumping, all to get away from his power. A couple of times, I stood my ground and parried the bolts with my sword so I could try to advance on him a little, but that required too much of my energy and strength; I wouldn't be able to keep that up for long. So, I resumed moving, jumping, tumbling as he made a show of his power, molding his bolts into daggers and birds and lightning.

At the edge of the circle, Alice kept demons at bay, away from me. An idea popped in my mind and I moved around the circle, putting Alice in my line of sight. Omi, she, and I formed an almost perfect equidistant triangle. As if sensing me, Alice looked over her shoulder and, praying for this ladies of Diana bond to be strong and magical, I hoped she could read my idea in my eyes. After half a second, she nodded and feigned ignorance by attacking the next demon that crossed her path.

I fished the throwing knives from my utility belt and, with a roar, lunged at Omi. Shock colored his face for one brief second before he created a shield in front of himself. His eyes on me, he didn't see as Alice charged him, not until the last second, before she leapt and flew at him. Another brief expression of shock took over Omi's face, but then he slammed a new shield down. Alice rolled out of the way right before hitting it, and raised her sword at him.

Then I was running, lunging at him myself. Without hesitation, without remorse, I pushed my hand out, letting my power, my magic out. White light burst from my hand, traveling in a quick wave toward Omi. The light hit him square in the chest, and he staggered back before falling to his knees.

Not wasting one second, I pulled my sword back before plunging it into his heart.

Eyes wide and mouth hanging open, Omi hit the floor with a dull thud. Alice straddled him and with two long daggers pierced his shoulders, making sure the weapons were buried deep enough that their tips stuck in the floor underneath him.

"That should hold him for a moment," Alice said, playing with her sword in her hand, ready to strike when he recovered from his wounds, which would be fast, since the damn man was a damn god.

I pressed my foot against his arm and pulled my sword out from his chest. He gasped, his face paling a little more, and thick red blood seeped out of the wound.

"I'll have my revenge," I snarled, taking the spear from his hands. For effect, I kicked his chin. His neck twisted with a sick crack.

"Go," Alice said as I turned away from the scene.

It wasn't easy to kill a god, and unfortunately I couldn't kill him. As for my revenge, he was probably thinking I would torture the hell out of him, or try to kill him for real. But that wasn't what was on my mind, as he would soon find out.

I rushed through the demons and lesser gods, trying to get to where Imha and her dozens of demons fought with Micah and Victor beside the reflective pool.

Always wanting attention and to be seen, Imha was standing on the large crystal blocks of the broken pool, making her an easy target.

It was now or never.

With the spear in hand, I dodged several demons and approached her. She was half-distracted with the battle against Micah and Victor, but I knew she wasn't stupid and she kept her senses open, making sure no one else could approach her.

So I didn't try to be stealthy.

"Hey, you bitch," I called.

Slowly, she turned to me.

I threw a dagger at her. She twisted her shoulders, to avoid being hit. Then I threw the spear.

It pierced her chest and she gasped, stunned.

I also gasped, stunned that she fell for the same trick I had used before.

Oh my God, it had worked. Imha stood immobile. It was as if she were frozen in place. Her arms by her side, her head staring ahead, her feet two or three inches from the floor.

It was as if *everyone* was frozen in place. The battle had hit a pause button while everyone stared at Imha and me, even the Lucent.

Imha looked down at the spear jutting from her chest. "But how ... what is this?"

"That's the Spear of Justice," I said, walking to her.

Omi let out a big scream, but Micah and Victor had him, and Sol growled in Ronen's and Izaera's grasps.

"Who do you think you are?" Imha snarled.

"Just a girl with a big ass weapon," I said.

I felt a force taking me over, a foreign power descending over me. I blinked and when I opened my eyes, it was as if I was a spectator, watching a movie.

I opened my mouth and a foreign voice said, "Imha, goddess of chaos, I hereby sentence you to—"

"No!" she screamed.

"—spend the next one hundred years in a special cell here in the Clarity Castle. During your sentence, your powers will be useless if you try anything against anyone from the

Creed, and outside that your powers will be lessened by fifty percent. When the one hundredth year comes, we'll meet again. If I decide you still didn't learn your lesson, I'll extend the time of your sentence for another one hundred years, and I'll do so until I find you trustworthy."

Several snorts and scoffs came from behind me.

The power in me made me move. I pulled the spear from her chest and she fell to her knees, breathing hard.

"No, no, no!" she sobbed.

I turned my back on her and threw the spear at Omi's chest. I repeated the same judgment, but Omi had the decency of not protesting or complaining.

When I pulled the spear from him, he wavered but didn't fall down.

Then I passed the similar judgment over Sol—instead of one hundred years, his sentence was cut in half. After all, he had been a puppet. But he had had choices, and he had made the wrong ones.

In a quick succession, I repeated the process with the lesser gods and goddesses that had sided with Imha and Omi. They too deserved to be punished for the evil they inflicted.

"Ronen, Izaera, please take them to the cells on the third floor," I said, once it seemed to be over. "Alice, please, help Lua."

They hustled into action.

And just like that, the force was gone and my knees wobbled.

Micah was by my side in less than a second, his arms around my waist. "I've got you, darling."

Around us, Maho and a couple of lesser gods rounded up the remaining demons, and Maho expelled them all to the island in Croatia—we didn't know what to do with all of them right now, but I certainly hoped the gods didn't kill anyone anymore.

Oddly enough, Lucent looked around. His glassy eyes scanned each one of the survivors, as if he was searching for our faces in a database and studying our records. Then he retreated to the pool, disappearing inside it. The two halves of the pool closed, but the destruction of Imha's explosion remained.

"What the hell?" I asked.

"He sensed the threat was over and went into sleep mode again," Micah said, slipping his arm from my waist to my shoulders and tucking me into his side.

Victor approached us, carrying a limping Ceris.

"So, I guess it's over, huh?" I said, not feeling the relief I thought I would feel.

"This war is over," Victor said. "We still have a lot to do."

I frowned. "But Imha and her demons are contained."

"True," Ceris said. She suppressed a cough. "But the world is still in chaos. Imha might be gone, but there are other threats out there."

Victor continued, "There are more demons hiding, and lesser gods and goddesses and other deities who didn't show up today on either side. We have to make sure they are following our rules and not gathering for a rebellion."

"By now the sun should be back and the weather and many other things should go back to normal," Micah said. "But in the last thirty years, many countries and nations have fallen, many governments were in disarray. We need to help the humans in any way we can."

I raised an eyebrow. "You plan on revealing yourselves to them?"

Victor shook his head. "No, but we can use our powers to

influence them, to help them make the right decisions to speed up the recovery. Once they have a good grip on it, we'll retreat and keep an eye from a distance."

"But first," Ceris paused, groaning. "We bring a healer to take care of our injured and we should rest."

I smiled at her. "And you need to rest."

She wrinkled her pretty nose. "Only after we're done here."

I shook my head. By the state of things inside the Clarity Castle, we wouldn't be done cleaning for days. I knew Victor would find a way to make her rest, though.

Meanwhile, Micah and I decided divide and conquer was the best approach, so after a quick kiss he and I went around the throne room, taking into account all that needed to be done, and the injured who needed immediate attention. It would be a long night.

AFTER HOURS HELPING AT THE CLARITY CASTLE, I FINALLY crossed the portal and went back to the villa. The portal let out at the reflective pool in the back garden.

My breath caught as I stared at the sky.

The black was receding, as if it had been clouds hanging above our heads this entire time, and the sun—the beautiful, bright, warm sun—was descending to hide behind the top of a hill.

The colors ...

Tears brimmed in my eyes. Blue and yellow and orange and even red splashed the canvas of the sky. Together with the green and purple of the garden, I was sure I had never seen a more beautiful sight in my entire life.

I sat at the edge of the pool and tilted my head back, trying to memorize each detail, each shade, each feeling coursing through me at this precious moment. Because this was the first time I was seeing the sun with my own eyes, and it would be the last.

Micah had been avoiding me since we separated to help with the wounded and repairs. I knew why he turned away each time I got close to him. I understood because I was feeling the same.

But a deal was a deal, and it was time to pay.

We won the war. There would be no immediate trouble. Yes, there still was a lot to be done to fix the world, to put it back together, but that wasn't my problem anymore. The gods and goddesses could do that without me. Now it was time for my family to come back—to a safer world, to a hopeful world—and live their lives.

I stood and went to search for Micah.

It was time for me to die.

39

THE CLARITY CASTLE AND THE VILLA IN ENGLAND LOOKED LIKE a hospital. There were cots spread everywhere and healers walking around going from deity to deity to make sure their wounds weren't fatal, or to speed up their already super healing.

The throne room had been cleared though, and Ceris, Levi, Izaera, Maho, Ronen, and I discussed our next steps.

The reflective pool was still destroyed, like the rest of the place. Our priority was to get everyone back to his or her full health, and then we would begin restoration.

After agreeing to take the less seriously wounded deities to the villa in England—and we made a note to seal the portal soon—Ceris decided it was time to bother me.

"Why isn't Nadine here?" Ceris asked, sitting on her throne. After spending half an hour with a healer, Ceris deemed she was feeling well enough to start helping too.

Groaning, I paced in front of my throne. "Don't."

"Oh, I forgot." Her tone dripped with sarcasm. "You're avoiding her."

"Stop," I hissed.

"Ceris," Levi said, his tone definite. "Stop bothering him."

"But it's true!" She became serious. "It's your responsibility. You can't avoid it forever. You know there are consequences."

"I know!" I shouted.

Fuck. It pained me to stay away from her, but yes, I had been avoiding Nadine. I always kept her aura on my radar, so I knew when she was coming, and I turned the other way. She was probably pissed at me, thinking I was running for two reasons. One, because I didn't love her anymore or two, because I wanted to delay the inevitable.

She was ready for the Soul Oath. I wasn't.

Letting out a sigh, I plopped down on my throne. "I can't … I can't lose her. I can't let her die."

"That's not your choice," Nadine said from behind me.

"Shit," I whispered. Apparently, I hadn't been doing a good job of checking for her aura. I stood and faced her. "Please, Nadine," I groaned. From the corner of my eye, I noticed Izaera, Maho, and Ronen leaving the room.

"No, Micah. You don't get to do this." She walked to me. "Please, don't do this to me. Don't make it harder than it has to be."

I ran a hand through my hair. "You can't ask that of me."

"Micah, I asked for this months ago and you agreed. I don't need to ask again; you just need to pay."

I groaned. "How can you be so fine about this?"

"I'm not!" she yelled. Then she continued, her voice even. "I'm not. But this is something I have to do. And I *will* do it. We will do it. Right now."

She was right. We couldn't delay the Soul Oath or we both would suffer unspeakable pains until both of us were too weak to finish what we started, and both of us died in torture. Well, that was how it was supposed to go. Being a god, I would probably survive, but it would still hurt a lot. I didn't mind the pain, though. What I minded was a life, an eternal life, without Nadine.

My eyes filled with tears. "Nadine ..."

She stepped into me and my arms went around her, holding her against me. I buried my face on her neck and inhaled deeply, trying to etch her sweet scent to my brain.

"I love you," she whispered in my ear. "I'll always love you."

"I ... I love you too," I said.

I moved my mouth to hers, kissing her soft and slow. It wasn't a deep, harsh kiss. It was a lingering, caring, longing kiss.

Nadine broke us apart and took three steps, probably knowing that if she didn't do it, I never would.

She wiped the tears from her eyes. "All right, what do we do?"

Pain seized my chest, but I pushed through it. For her, I endured it.

I conjured a dagger in my hand and pricked her index finger with it, drawing blood. I did the same with mine. I took her palm and smeared my blood on it, then did the same with her blood on my palm. Next, I placed her bloodstained palm over my heart and my hand over her chest.

"Ready?" I asked, my voice alien even to me.

"Yes," she said, loud and clear. How she was hanging on like that, knowing that she would die any second, baffled me. "My Soul Oath is complete."

"Your Soul Oath is complete." I held my breath.

Nothing happened.

I clasped Nadine's shoulders. "You're still alive," I said in wonder. "Are you feeling okay?"

She nodded. Then her eyes widened and she shook her head. "I feel ... dizzy and weak." Her knees shook and I caught her before she could hit the floor.

"No, no, no." I knelt on the floor with her in my arms.

"It's okay," she whispered. She rested her hand on my face and tried to smile. "I'm happy we had a few days together."

I kissed her hand, my eyes on her. Please, please ... I didn't even know to whom I should pray. "Nadine ..."

She took a slow breath and her body grew heavier in my arms. It was as if her batteries were running out. "Be happy, Micah."

Nadine closed her eyes and her hand fell to the side.

"No." I knew what was coming, but I still couldn't believe she was gone. I just couldn't. I rested my head on her chest and tried to listen to her heart. Nothing. There was nothing. Her heart wasn't beating.

I screamed.

Levi's hand squeezed my shoulder. "I'm sorry, brother."

I jerked my shoulder, making him release me. "No! It's not over!" I stood with Nadine in my arms. "I'm the god of death. I can block her soul's entrance to the underworld. I can bring her back. I can do something!"

Ceris approached me. "She's gone, Mitrus. By the Soul Oath. You can't cheat it."

"But you can honor her," Levi said. "By doing what you promised. Give her body to us, we'll prepare a proper ceremony for her, meanwhile you can bring her family back to life."

"No!" I roared, taking several steps away from them. "No. I'm not ready to let go."

"Mitrus," Ceris started.

I knelt on the floor again, holding Nadine. I buried my face in her hair and cried like I had never cried in my thousands of years.

"Oh, darling," I whispered between sobs. "I love you. I will always love you. Forever."

Her body trembled in my arms and I pulled away just enough to look at her face, to her arms, to examine her. When I was human, I remembered reading somewhere that some dead bodies jerk as if they had been electrocuted. It was a normal response. And yet, I couldn't help but hope.

"Nadine?" I asked in a low, careful voice.

I dared not breathe while I stared at her for a long time, hoping, wishing the tremor in her body meant more.

A strong and powerful aura exploded from inside her.

I gasped and stared at Levi and Ceris as they gaped at Nadine.

Nadine's eyes fluttered and she moaned. I let out a loud, happy gasp. Ceris and Levi rushed to my side.

"Hi," she croaked, opening her beautiful green eyes and staring straight at me.

I touched her face. I caressed her cheek. She was here. She was alive! "You're ... you're ..."

She wrinkled her nose. "I'm Diana. I'm Diana?" Her voice was still weak, but it was *her* voice!

"By the Everlast," Levi muttered somewhere from beside us.

"How ... how is this possible?" Ceris asked in a shocked tone.

"Right now, I don't care." I wound my arms around Nadine and pulled her to me. "I can't even begin to describe how happy I am right now." I inhaled deeply, savoring her scent. Gods, she was here with me.

"My sister ... oh, my beautiful sister," she whispered.

I pulled back and saw her eyes filled with tears. "Your sister?"

She extended one hand to me and I took it without hesitation. A cold seeped from her skin to mine, bringing forth hidden memories, memories I had no idea had been buried inside me. Nadine was Diana, the goddess of courage and wisdom, and she had had a twin sister, Neena, the goddess of justice and honesty. When Neena fell in love with a human, she abdicated being a goddess to be with the man she loved, passing on her powers to Nadine—Diana. That was how she had become the goddess of courage, justice, wisdom, and honesty.

"By the Everlast," I muttered, suddenly overwhelmed with the burst of new information. "That's ... how could we forget you?"

"Forget her?" Ceris asked. "What are you talking about?"

Nadine pulled her hand from mine and gave it to Ceris. The goddess gasped. Then she repeated the process with Levi.

Wiping at her tears, Nadine pulled away to look at me. "I'm happy to be alive too, but honestly, I'm curious about a few things."

The Fates popped in behind us.

"We can explain," Nay said.

40

NADINE

MICAH AND I STOOD, BUT HE KEPT ME TUCKED INTO HIM. IT seemed he needed to touch me, to feel me, to be sure I was really here. I wasn't complaining.

"You finally found out who you really are," Mani said.

"About that," I started. "Did Ceris know who I was? Am? Or would be?" It was all so confusing.

"No, she didn't," Mani answered.

"We merely pointed her in the right direction," Nay said, looking at Ceris. The goddess only nodded.

"Oh-kay," I muttered. "Next question. Micah's and Victor's soul found new hosts just a few years after their deaths. How come my soul stayed adrift for thousands and thousands of years?"

Mani took a step back. "You were the first goddess to find out what the Black Thorn could do. Sad and lost after your sister's death, and against your own principles, you created one to kill yourself. Since you were out of the Everlasting Circle, you knew your death wouldn't affect the balance of the world, so you did it. Because you couldn't endure eternity without your sister, you killed yourself without remorse."

"You caught even us by surprise," Lavni said. "We felt your soul drifting away, and at first, we didn't know what to do. So we imprisoned your spirit, hoping someday we would be able to use it."

"Several millennia passed," Nay said. "Then Mitrus and Levi killed each other."

"With the help of Imha and Omi," Micah added under his breath.

Nay ignored him and went on. "Their souls found new hosts on their own, and we realized we could set your soul free again and guide it to the right host."

"But it wasn't easy to find the right host, until we sensed a tiny little thing forming in your mother's womb," Nay said. "We knew you were the one destined to become Diana."

It was too much to take on at once. So ... I had always been Nadine *and* Diana? That sounded so crazy and impossible. But after all I had seen and lived through these past few months, I had to come up with a new definition for crazy and impossible.

I let out a long breath and asked my next question. "What about my sister? Where is she? Why hasn't she come back like I did?"

"Neena is happy in the underworld with the love of her life," Nay said. "She abdicated her immortality to be with her lover, thus dying a mortal's death. Because of that, her soul—her mortal soul—went directly to the underworld and she wo—"

"She won't be back," I whispered. A heavy feeling revolved in my chest—a painful longing I was sure would never dull. How could I suddenly miss someone so badly when minutes ago I didn't even know about her?

"Any more questions?" Mani asked, her tone flat and bored.

That jerked me out from the pain within. "Yes," I said. "How was I forgotten by the other gods and goddesses and why?"

"Time is a funny thing," Lavni said.

"So many years passed from the time of your death, that first the tales of your life became a legend, and then you were simply forgotten," Mani said.

"The truth is, you were always in the back of the gods' and goddesses' minds, but since they hadn't heard your name in so long, it never came forth," Nay said. "Until now."

"I have one question," Ceris spoke up. The Fates turned to her. "Levi and Mitrus remembered who they were when we were at the Cathedral Rock. Shouldn't Nadine have remembered herself then?"

"And we became full gods when we found our scepters," Victor added. "Nadine found her spear and didn't become Diana until now."

Mani answered, "Nadine didn't remember she was Diana at Cathedral Rock because it's a portal to the Clarity Castle, which is a part of the Everlasting Circle, and Nadine wasn't a part of the creed."

"As for touching the spear and not becoming Diana then, well there are things not even we know the answers to," Lavni said.

"But we do have a couple of theories," Nay said. "We think Nadine was unconsciously so against the idea of being something more than a normal human—"

"Against or just scared," Mani added quickly.

"—that her powers and her soul were tucked in her too deep, locked away, never to be found," Nay explained.

"Until the Soul Oath killed Nadine and, before her mortal soul could drift away, Diana's soul awoke and absorbed her mortal one."

"Wow," I whispered, feeling overwhelmed.

Micah tensed beside me. "So, the Soul Oath is paid?"

"Yes," Mani said.

"And I'm immortal now?" I asked.

"Yes," Nay said.

I sucked in a sharp breath, needing time to process such news. I had been so used to the idea of dying, it would take me some time to get used to the fact that now I was going to live forever.

Holy shit, I was immortal!

And my family would come back to life soon, and I would see them again!

"Thank you for winning the war and imprisoning Imha and Omi," Nay said, catching my attention. She looked pointedly at each one of us.

And just like that they poofed out.

A new wave of happiness filled my chest as Micah embraced me and spun me around. "You're here."

With my arms around his neck, I laughed. "I'm here."

He set me down and stared at me, as if he was afraid I would disappear if he stopped looking at me. I pressed a hand to his chest, just above his heart and felt his strong heart beating against my palm. Which reminded me ...

I snaked my hand under his shirt and placed my palm over the center of the poisoned web spreading through his chest.

"Darling?" he asked, a question in his eyes. He lifted his shirt and looked down at where my hand met his warm skin.

And I healed him. Just like that.

Micah gasped as the dark web faded from his skin. "What ...?"

I shrugged. "Healing powers. One of the advantages of being Diana, I guess."

Without hesitation, Micah leaned down and kissed me. It started like our last kiss. Slow and soft. Just a brushing of our lips. A promise. A remembrance. Micah startled me then by claiming my mouth with his and deepening the kiss, making me wish he could kiss me enough to leave a bit of his soul in me.

"So." Victor cleared his throat.

Micah raised his hand and was about to throw a bolt at his feet, but I grabbed his arm and didn't let him.

We turned to Victor.

"To celebrate that Diana is back and will live forever with us ..." Victor waved his hand to an empty spot beside the thrones. Bright lights moved like spiral snakes until a new throne appeared in its place. "This one is for you, Diana."

I gasped. "Are you sure?"

Ceris smiled at me. "Of course. You might not have been a part of the creed before, but after all you did for us, you sure are part of it now."

Slowly, I walked to *my* throne and sat down. I rested my hands on the armrests and leaned against the high back.

"I could get used to this," I said.

Micah sat on the throne beside mine and reached out, taking my hand. "Welcome to the Everlasting Circle, Diana."

EPILOGUE

NADINE

I WENT AROUND THE LIVING ROOM, MAKING SURE EVERYTHING was where it was supposed to be. Then, I went to the kitchen and opened all the cabinets and the fridge, making sure there was enough food, plates, glasses, and pots and pans. I looked over the steak in the oven, making sure it was cooking well. When I left the kitchen to go upstairs to the bedrooms, Micah stepped in front of me.

"You already checked the place, darling. Twice. You know it's ready."

A shuddering breath escaped me. "I know."

But it was all I could do to try and keep calm—and it wasn't working.

After the Soul Oath, Micah and I decided it was best to bring back my family after we found a good place for them to live. We searched the United States for a place that hadn't been too destroyed by the war. We found a small town in Virginia, which didn't seem too bad. As best as we could, we helped the townsfolk clean it up and rebuild and fix everything in need. In a couple of days, more people arrived, probably hearing the town was prospering.

Micah and I chose a nice house big enough—but not too big—for my family. With four small children, my parents would need a bigger house than they were used to. We fixed the house, decorated, stocked the kitchen, and made sure the basics were all there. My family wouldn't need anything else to live comfortably for a while.

More importantly, Micah and I agreed that right before they came back to life we had to change their memories of what happened.

This was the hardest part.

The new story was that Troy hadn't been born after me and had died young. He would now be the last baby—otherwise it would be hard to explain how he hadn't aged like the rest of them. Also, they would remember my visit before we were all captured, but they wouldn't remember the demons chasing us. Their memory would be of me going back to school, where I inexplicably found a nice job that paid well, and I was able to buy them this new house in this nice town. We had even found a job for my father with a local farmer, which paid relatively well and would allow my mother to stay home with my siblings. Moreover, if they ever needed more money, I could simply send it to them, saying that with my new job I was practically rich and could afford spending money on them.

Thankfully, they wouldn't remember much of the violence, the hunger, the despair.

Micah pulled me into his arms and I rested my cheek on his chest, relishing the strong beat of his heart. "It's okay to be nervous, darling."

"It's just … I know each time I look at them, I'll remember every terror they lived through." That *we* lived through.

Micah kissed the top of my head. "It's all gone now." He put a hand under my chin and tilted my head up. "Besides, now you're a powerful goddess. Nothing is going to happen. You can protect them now."

He was right. If I had been Diana back then I might have been able to free them from Imha and Omi, and they never would have died. I vowed never to let them suffer again.

"How are you going to do it?" I had no idea if he had to open a portal from here to the underworld, or if he had to go there and pick them personally, or how the hell it worked.

"I'm gonna invoke them and they will simply walk through that door—" He pointed to the front door. "—as if they had just arrived from their trip."

I kissed his cheek. "Thank you."

He turned his head and kissed me on the lips. "Anytime, darling."

Hands intertwined, Micah and I turned to the door.

"Are you ready?" he asked.

I nodded, words failing me.

The front door opened and my father walked in with a big smile on his face. He was carrying two big suitcases, one on each hand.

"Nad!" he exclaimed. "It's so good to see you."

"Hi, Dad." My voice broke and my eyes filled with tears.

My father grunted with the weight of the bags as he walked in the house.

Micah let go of me and went to him. "Let me get that for you, sir." He picked up both suitcases from my father.

Then my mother walked into the house with little Troy in her arms. A sob ripped through my chest. It was too much for me. I ran to them, and embraced them both, hooking my arms around their necks and pulling them close.

"My goodness, Nad." My mother laughed. "I didn't know you missed us that much."

"Oh, I missed you. So much," I whispered.

My mother kissed my cheek. "We missed you too, dear."

I stifled a sob. She was talking about the last time she thought she saw me, when I was visiting them after New York City was destroyed. Only Micah and I would ever know I was talking about their deaths.

I took Troy from my mother's arms. He was so little, so perfect, so beautiful. A tear spilled from my eyes.

My father stepped back and glanced at the guy standing behind me. Serious, my father extended his hand to Micah. "Hi. I'm Nadine's father."

Micah took my father's hand and shook it. "I'm Micah, Nadine's boyfriend."

My mother raised an eyebrow at me. "He's cute." She turned her shoulder slightly and gave me a thumbs up, hidden from view by her body. I laughed at the absurdity of this situation. A month ago, I was crying because they were dead, and now I was talking about boys with my parents.

"Boyfriend, huh?" My father glanced at me.

My cheeks flushed. "Yeah, Micah is my boyfriend." The word was still so strange to say out loud. It was so strange, period. Immortals had boyfriends and girlfriends? That sounded so ridiculous.

Micah flashed me one of his old cocky grins. God, how I loved that handsome face.

"Aaaah!" a scream cut through our peace and Nicole, Teddie, and Tommy burst through the front door, running into the living room and barreling into us.

When they saw me, they stopped.

"Nad!" cried Nicole. She threw herself at my legs and held on tight.

My mother picked up Troy as I swallowed another sob and knelt beside Nicole. I held her in my arms, then Teddie and Tommy threw themselves over us and we all fell on the floor.

I laughed, a real loud, belly laugh. I saw Micah watching us, a smile on his lips. His eyes met mine and my chest swelled. This moment right here with my father, my mother, Troy, Nicole, Teddie, Tommy, and Micah. All of us well and smiling. This moment was perfect. I wished it could be like this forever.

For Micah and me, it would be forever. My family wasn't immortal though. I knew they would die someday, but I would make sure they lived a happy and long life before the end came. It would be hard, but I would let them go in peace this time.

I sighed, pushing those thoughts away. I hoped I wouldn't have to dwell on that for many, many years.

"Kids, kids," my father called. My siblings raised their heads. "Let your sister breathe."

"Why don't you take your things to your bedrooms, huh?" my mother said, handing each of them a small backpack.

"Where's our bedroom?" Teddie asked.

"Upstairs," I said. "You'll find your names on the doors."

They raced up the stairs, shouting and giggling the entire time.

Micah and my father went back outside to bring the rest of their things inside. It wasn't much, unfortunately, and I went to the kitchen with my mother and Troy to check on dinner.

"It's almost ready," I said, closing the oven's door. I turned and found her smiling at me. "What?"

"You. You look so good, so strong, so well. I'm happy for you."

"Thanks. I feel happy."

"Hello?" a new voice called from the front of the house.

"In the kitchen," I said, smiling.

Ceris, Victor, Alice, Keisha, and Morgan entered the kitchen. My mother's eyes widened. Surely, she wasn't expecting this many people to appear in her new kitchen.

"Micah was outside and told us to come in," Victor said.

"It's okay." I turned to my mother. "Mom, these are my friends." I told her their names and they all shook hands. "They'll be staying for dinner with us."

My mother smiled. "Of course."

Soon we called everyone for dinner. Micah and my father paused the boring task of moving in, and the kids came rushing from upstairs like a mini tornado.

As we sat at the long dining table—with extra chairs from the kitchen's table so we all could fit, barely, at the table—my mother served the kids; they couldn't stop talking about having their own bedrooms, their own beds, and so many toys. They looked so happy that I thought my heart would burst.

My mother talked to Ceris about kids; Keisha and Alice looked like they were expecting orders from me—still trying to get used to the fact that they both were *my* ladies—and my father talked to Victor and Morgan about farms and crops.

Under the table, Micah took my hand in his and intertwined our fingers. I looked at him and he was smiling at me. I leaned my head against his shoulder and I looked at all the people I loved around the table.

Even Keisha and Morgan were here, after we finally convinced them Micah could trade their souls for two of the people Imha had killed. It sounded so evil, but she had killed millions. And they were family. We needed them here.

Moreover, I knew Raisa and Olivia, my friends from college, were doing well. They had lived through the worst and now they and their families would live in a better world. I hoped to see them again, at least one more time.

One person I knew I would see more times was Neena. Since becoming Diana, Micah had taken me to the underworld twice to see her. The first time was a tear-fest, but on my second visit we were able to talk as we used to, several millennia ago. It was good to know I could still reach her, even if she was tucked away from this world.

"It makes me happy to see you this happy," Micah whispered in my ear. I let out a huge, relieved sigh, and he kissed the top of my head.

My smile was wide and true, and my heart could burst any moment with such happiness. I couldn't imagine a more perfect moment.

THANK YOU!

Thank you for reading *Everlasting Circle*!

I hope you have enjoyed the entire series as much I liked writing it.

Reviews are very important for authors. If you liked my book, please consider leaving a review on amazon and/or on goodreads, please!

Don't forget to sign up for my Newsletter to find out about new releases, cover reveals, giveaways, and more: http://bitly.com/JuHNL

If you want to see exclusive teasers, help me decide on covers, read excerpts, talk about books, etc, join my reader group on Facebook: https://www.facebook.com/groups/JulianasClub/

ABOUT THE AUTHOR

While USA Today Bestselling Author Juliana Haygert dreams of being Wonder Woman, Buffy, or a blood elf shadow priest, she settles for the less exciting—but equally gratifying—life as a wife, a mother, and an author. Thousands of miles away from her former home in Brazil, she now resides in North Carolina and spends her days writing about kick-ass heroines and the heroes who drive them crazy.

Subscribe to her mailing list to receive emails of announcement, events, and other fun stuff related to her writing and her books: www.bit.ly/JuHNL

For more information:

www.julianahaygert.com

Breaking Free (Book 1)

Breaking Away (Book 2)

Breaking Through (Book 3)

Standalones

Playing Pretend

Captured Love

Dazzle Me